Romance in a Flash:

Mini Love Stories You Can Read on Your Coffee Break

By
Gayle Leigh Gwinn

Table of Contents

Author's Note..................................1

To Kiss a Stranger.........................2

Most Valyoobl...............................8

Gold Digger.................................13

Slaying Dragons.............................18

Bodacious Flirtatious.......................25

Taken Out of Con-TEXT.......................29

The Condensed Version.......................34

Party Girl..................................40

Stealing His Heart..........................45

Fool Me, April..............................50

Marty's Heart...............................55

The Right Fit...............................60

The Easter Basket...........................64

No Picnic...................................71

Moon Dance..................................75

The Heart Tree..............................75

First Flush of Love.........................88

Boomer......................................93

Walleyes....................................99

The Sweetest Day............................104

Bizzy Bea...................................111

The Lone Wolf...............................117

A Haunting Refrain..........................123

Million Dollar Goofball.....................136

Love on Aisle 7...................................143

Birthday Kiss.....................................147

Desert Dreams..................................123

The Christmas Game........................154

Santa's Lap.......................................158

A Last Love Story.............................164

About the Author.............................170

Author's Note

Dear Reader,

This is a collection of mini romances, approximately 1000-1600 words each, that can be read in as little as ten to fifteen minutes, ideal for those of you on coffee breaks, and for those of you who love romance but have little time to read.

Some of them are quirky; some have serious elements (I feature stories centered around: a congenital eye disorder; Asperger's; Thalidomide birth defects and war injuries; and an endangered animal). Some have children in them, and some do not. Most of my characters are youthful, a few of them are in their late thirties, and one couple is retirement age. I've also included stories about the usual holidays and one that's a bit unusual. I hope all of these stories are enjoyable to everyone.

I also hope you will send me your feedback via my email: **shariannegaylee@gmail.com**. If there's any story that you particularly like, perhaps I'll rework it into a longer short story, novelette, novella or novel.

So, grab yourself a delicious cup of your favorite coffee (or tea) and delight in a quick love story while you sip.

Bottoms up!

Gayle Leigh Gwinn

To Kiss a Stranger

[Rikki's friend Leah bets her $50 that she can't walk up to a total stranger and kiss him as the New Year rings in.]

Rikki Reed was tired, tired of living her life alone. Her fortieth birthday was tomorrow, New Year's Eve. She used to joke that everyone celebrated her birthday, but now she didn't want to acknowledge it, let alone go out, like her best friend, Leah, wanted her to.

She sighed and spoke into the receiver of her iPhone. "Leah, I just don't feel like celebrating this year. If I had a man, I might, but it's been you and me, sans men, every year, for the past five years. It's like we're both cursed or something."

"We're not cursed, Rikki. How can you say that? You're just too picky—Picky Rikki—who could have had a man at her side every year on her birthday for the past five years, *if* she hadn't dumped them before the day arrived."

"Leah..." Rikki tried to interrupt.

Leah ignored her and continued, "*I* don't feel like I'm cursed, and I haven't been nearly as lucky as you in the romance department. I had a good man six years ago, and it wasn't his fault he was killed in that foggy freeway pileup. When he got on the road, it was clear, then the fog drifted in. It wasn't even forecasted. Andrew would never have driven in those conditions under normal circumstances. And I know he'd want me to find someone as great as he was, so I'm believing it will happen."

"For *you*, maybe—at least you've had true love once in your life. But for me—there's a difference between dating a lot of loser frogs and being lucky enough to find a prince. I am SO done with it."

"Oh, come on, Rikki, you can't give up on me." There was silence for a second or two, then Leah said, "I've got a great idea! Pow! It just hit me. What if, at the stroke of midnight, you just go for it and kiss the first guy you see standing alone at the party tonight? How could that be any worse than kissing the losers you've already kissed?"

"Are you nuts?" Rikki yelled. "I'm not kissing some stranger. Besides, just because a guy is by himself doesn't mean he's alone. What if his date just happened to go to the restroom or went off to get a refill? Then, not only would I feel ridiculous because I was such an idiot, I'd probably get my eyes scratched out when the girlfriend returned. No thanks."

"I dare you."

"Nope. Not doing it."

"I double-dog dare you."

"Forget it, Leah," Rikki said flatly.

"I triple-dog dare you!" Leah yelled, as if they were ten years old and had just watched the scene in *A Christmas Story* where the stupid kid licked a frozen flagpole and got his tongue stuck to it.

"Leah..." Rikki said, exasperated.

"Okay, if daring won't work, how 'bout I pay you to do it? I'll give you fifty bucks to kiss the first guy who's standing alone in your vicinity at midnight."

Well, who was Rikki to refuse fifty dollars—especially when she was short just that amount for her upcoming rent, and Leah knew it.

"Fine. You win."

"And no quick peck on the lips, either. This has to be a full-fledged lip lock, or no fifty bucks. And I'll be watching."

"Alright, alright. But if I catch mono or strep throat or something else, you'll pay the doctor bill, too."

Leah chortled with glee. "Okay, you're on! Bruce wouldn't invite any sickies to his party in the first place, and if someone did show up sniffling, he'd send them home."

Bruce, a mutual gay friend of theirs, was unusual. He was so likeable, he had scads of hetero male friends as well as a zillion gay ones. Which made Rikki pause.

"What if it's a gay guy I end up kissing? Won't that defeat the purpose?"

"Well, I guess we'll just have to take our chances. I'll meet you at your place for the taxi ride over tomorrow at six, okay?"

"Okay," Rikki answered glumly. Six hours of party before she could get the stupid kiss over with and escape. Oh, joy.

The next evening, Leah showed up at her door at 5:45 with a present and a bottle of champagne.

"Leah, I told you no presents. Especially not when you're paying me $50 to pull this crazy stunt."

Leah pushed past her, put the present and the champagne on the bench in the foyer, and wheeled around to pull Rikki into a hug. "Happy Birthday, girlfriend. You'll see...this one will be the best ever, and to start it off right, let's have a quick glass of bubbly. The cabbie said he'd wait for us."

She released Rikki and headed straight for the kitchen, giving her friend no chance to argue. Returning with two flutes and a dish towel, Leah proceeded to expertly pop the cork and pour the bubbly. "To my best bud for the past twenty years, and may we be best buds for twenty more and twenty more and twenty more—"

"Jeez, how long do you think we're gonna live, anyway?" Rikki interrupted, laughing as they clinked glasses. She was glad to have Leah as a best friend. As someone who was basically alone in the world, Rikki knew better than most how valuable good friends were.

"Come on, then. Let's get this party over with," Leah said.

"Let's get this party *started,* you mean!"

Bruce's condo was jam-packed when they arrived, even at such an early hour, which again, pointed to his enormous popularity. After he ushered them in and told Rikki, "Happy Birthday, girl! We're sharing this party, you know," he led the way to the buffet he'd spread out in the dining room, air-kissed their cheeks and left them on their own.

The huge array of tasty finger foods and the free-flowing drinks did a lot to ease Rikki's discomfort and put her in a party mood. Several of her other friends were there, and she spent the night gabbing with them. Time flew, and before she knew it, her birthday was nearing its end.

"Alright, everyone, ten minutes to midnight!" Bruce announced into the deejay's microphone.

Leah, who had gone off with an accountant she'd met around nine o'clock, suddenly appeared at Rikki's side with the guy in tow. "Are you looking for your victim yet?" she whispered into her ear.

"I'll find someone, don't worry."

"Well, you sure did leave it 'til the last minute, didn't you? Guess you don't want that fifty bucks very much."

To be honest, Rikki had been so engrossed in catching up with an old friend, Celeste, whom she hadn't seen in a good ten years, she'd forgotten all about the dare... until Leah showed back up. Realizing how careless she'd been not to scope things out sooner, she anxiously scanned the room for a likely kissee.

Then she saw him. Tall, dark, and ruggedly handsome, he didn't appear to be one of Bruce's more "intimate" friends. He was standing just ten feet away, and he looked straight at Rikki, as though he felt her gaze. When their eyes met, a zing shot through Rikki, and she started moving toward him of her own accord.

"One minute to midnight!" Bruce whooped, and the crowd went crazy. They started hollering the sixty-second countdown, tooting horns, blowing on kazoos, stamping their feet, clapping their hands and generally making any kind of ruckus they could. Someone stepped in front of her, and Rikki lost sight of the man she had intended to kiss.

"Twenty-five...twenty-four...twenty-three..."

Dodging around the rather heavyset woman, Rikki wove through several more partygoers who'd moved in closer for the revelry.

"Ten...nine...eight..."

Darn! He must have moved. She couldn't see him anywhere. She wasn't going to make it. Oh, well, there went the rest of the rent money.

"Five...four...three..."

Rikki sighed with frustration then felt herself being grabbed from behind and swung around. All she saw was a head of dark hair before a pair of lips swooped down to claim hers.

"Two...one..."

"HAPPY NEW YEAR!"

Rikki was so busy returning the greatest kiss she'd ever had she didn't even notice it was after midnight.

"Hey, you two, break it up!" Leah ordered a full minute later. They ignored her. She chuckled, stuck a crisp fifty dollar bill into the back pocket of Rikki's slacks and sauntered off.

Most Valyoobl

[Molly decides to value herself more after reading her daughter's note to the "Tuth Faree" and gets a new job and a new man in the process.]

Molly tiptoed into her six-year-old's bedroom with her keychain flashlight in one hand and a dollar in the other hand. The incisor that had been wiggling precariously back and forth for over a week had come out when Ashlyn bit into a fried chicken leg at dinner.

As she started to slip the bill under Ashlyn's pillow Molly felt a piece of paper. Withdrawing it, she crept out of the room and down the hall to her own room where she could read it without awakening her daughter.

Deer Tuth Faree,

This is my most valyoobl tuth, so I am asking 100 dollers for it.

Thank you,

Ashlyn

Molly giggled at her daughter's spelling attempts and at her audacity. A hundred dollars! Whoever heard of a tooth fairy giving a kid that kind of money for a tooth? And what would a six-year-old do with a hundred dollars, anyway?

Then she sobered. She wished she *could* give her daughter the amount she had requested. That kind of self-assurance shouldn't be destroyed.

And what she wouldn't give to borrow a chunk of Ashlyn's confidence for herself, especially where men were concerned.

But it seemed Molly just didn't have what it took to attract the man of her dreams. Fifteen years of adulthood and all she'd drawn to her was a string of bad relationships, the one with Ashlyn's father being the worst. The only good thing to come out of her disastrous six-month marriage to him was Ashlyn.

Molly hadn't dated since, preferring to focus her energies on child-raising. If Ashlyn's note was anything to go by, she was a lot more successful in parenting than she'd realized.

Which made it imperative that she find a way to get that "100 dollers". Well, it wouldn't happen tonight. Molly penned a note from the "tuth faree" back to Ashlyn.

Dear Ashlyn,

I don't have that kind of cash on me right now. No kid has ever valued their tooth that much before. Here's a dollar. I.O.U. $99.

Sincerely,

Tooth Fairy

After she put the note and the money under Ashlyn's pillow, Molly snuck back to her bed and lay awake a long time, planning how to get the extra cash she owed her daughter and also pondering Ashlyn's valuation of herself, aware that it was this factor that was prompting her to give her little girl what she asked for.

Hmm, what would happen if she started acting like she esteemed herself as much as Ashlyn did? Yawning, Molly decided, as she entered slumberland, that she had nothing to lose and everything to gain by giving it a shot.

New mindset firmly in place, the next day Molly entered the bakery that had a "Help Wanted" sign in its window and asked for an application. If she could work the part-time 4:00 a.m.-8:00 a.m. baking shift, she could keep her regular job and have the extra money in two weeks, even after paying a sitter.

Tapping her pen against her chin at the last question on the application the girl at the counter had handed her, "Why do you want to work for us?" she finally wrote, "Although your bakery offers great products, I can bake them even better!" and turned it in.

Later that same day, her cell phone rang. "Can you come in for an interview in the next hour?" a male voice inquired.

Molly glanced at the clock. She didn't get off until 5:00 and it was only 2:00. "Sure!" she replied, remembering to act as if the job was already hers. She'd get her boss to let her leave early somehow.

Arriving at the bakery fifteen minutes beforehand, Molly strode into the place as though she owned it. A man she hadn't seen before came through the swinging doors when the bell tinkled. "Molly?" he asked.

"You betcha!" Molly held her head high and her hand out.

He shook it and she felt a sizzle all the way up her arm. "I'm Ryan Flannery, owner and chief baker. Come on back."

After seating her in a chair opposite him in his cramped office, Ryan Flannery steepled his fingers and quirked an auburn brow at her. "I'm just curious. What makes you think you can bake better—without experience—than me, a culinary arts graduate?"

Molly felt heat climb her neck. Uh-oh. She'd gone too far with that stupid boast. Still, she had to pull this off, not just for Ashlyn, but for herself, too. "I just meant that my assistance would free you to unleash your creative talents. 'Bake' was my cutesy way of saying 'make'. I can 'make' things better by helping you."

Ryan's brow went down. He smiled. "In that case,

you've got yourself a job."

Molly exhaled slowly so as not to give away the relief she felt.

Two weeks later, she'd already had a first date with Ryan, and things were going better in that department than they ever had before. Placing $99 from her first paycheck under Ashlyn's pillow, she thought, *That "most valyoobl tuth" was worth every cent.*

Gold Digger

[A convenience store clerk is astounded when a handsome stranger makes a small purchase, drops a $100 bill on the counter and tells her to keep the change. When they begin to date, Natasha is accused of being a gold digger, and Lonny puts the woman in her place.]

"Where am I gonna get an extra $150?" Natasha wailed as she examined the invoice from the electric company. "This is way more than I expected, and I can't even pay the other bills I've got."

"Tell me about it," her friend Charli agreed. "Working here barely keeps me off the streets. Ever since the mine shut down, this place has been like a ghost town."

Both women were so engrossed in their conversation they didn't notice the customer who had come in and was browsing the aisles until he moved up to the counter. "I'm headed into the back to stock the cooler," Charli said as Natasha rang up his purchase.

"That'll be $8.80, please," Natasha told the man, smiling as she bagged his energy drink and sandwich. She couldn't help noticing his blond curls and sky-blue eyes.

He handed her $100. Someone around here actually had that kind of cash? Amazing!

"Keep the change," he told her.

"What!?" she stared at him in total shock.

He smiled. "I couldn't help overhearing that you're having money worries. Call it my good deed for the day."

"I can't take your money, sir!" Natasha protested.

"What's with the 'sir' bit?" he teased, enjoying her discomfiture. "I'm not a knight."

"Oh, but this gesture's just the kind a chivalrous knight would make," Natasha rallied, still trying to hand him his change. "While I appreciate it... no thanks."

He merely picked up his bag and sauntered out of the store, whistling.

"I don't believe it!" Natasha squealed once he'd driven off.

"What don't you believe?" Charli asked, emerging from the back.

"That guy only owed $8.80, but he handed me a hundred dollar bill and told me to keep the change!"

"Get out! He gave up ninety-one dollars and twenty cents, just like that?" Charli's eyes were huge. "He must not be from around here, then. Have you ever seen him before?"

"No."

"Then I'll bet he was just passing through. Too bad. I wouldn't mind getting the chance to wait on him, myself."

Natasha felt a pang at Charli's assessment. *She* wouldn't have minded getting the chance to know him, and money had nothing to do with it. Those baby blues of his had really grabbed her. Living in the Sierra Nevadas had advantages—spectacular scenery, for one—but it also had disadvantages—like few available men. The ones who were around were too rough for Natasha's taste: mostly hunters and fishermen who chewed tobacco and guzzled beer in the local saloons.

She pocketed her windfall, silently thanking the man. At least she could almost pay her electric bill now. Best to count her blessings and let it go.

During the next few weeks, everyone in the little Mother Lode town was abuzz with excitement, especially the men who'd once worked the mine. "He's gonna reopen the Lucky Strike!" Wally, a grizzled guy in his fifties who always hit on her, told Natasha.

"Who's reopening it?" she asked.

"Some guy from the Bay Area. Came up here a coupla weeks ago and bought it cash outright."

Could it be my rescuing knight? Natasha wondered. His face had loomed large in all her fantasies of late.

The very next day, the object of her thoughts came into the mini-mart and tried to get her to keep the change again. This time, she put the money in the bag with his purchases. "You've really got to stop this," she protested.

"No, I don't," he gazed into her eyes, "but I will if you go out with me."

"I don't go out with strangers." Natasha's heartbeat accelerated to about 150 mph.

"Name's Lonny. Lonny Lockhart." He whipped his hand out to capture hers. "What's yours?"

"N-Natasha," she stammered, heart rate off the charts at his touch.

Lonny shook her hand. "Now we're not strangers, so how about dinner after you get off? I hear that Italian place up the street has fantastic food."

"Okay," the word popped out.

* * *

Over the next two months, they grew steadily closer, yet when Natasha asked Lonny where he was from, trying to ascertain whether he was the town's mysterious new benefactor, he insisted, "No past details; let's just enjoy the moment."

So, Natasha showed him the best Witcomb's Creek had to offer and didn't worry about it.

"Gold digger!" a woman dressed in garb circa 1849 hissed when she passed her on the plank sidewalk of the preserved gold rush town.

Lonny stiffened beside Natasha. "Hey, lady!" he called. The woman who'd been so nasty pivoted.

"Natasha's not the gold digger, *I* am. I tried to give her some of my wealth, and she wouldn't take it. Remember that."

Natasha recalled the huge nugget brought up from the mine last month that put the town squarely back on the map. Her heart couldn't begin to compare, but she offered it to him anyway, right in front of the woman.

"Thank you, my love," she told him with her sweetest smile.

"'My love', eh? Now that's real gold, sweetheart!" Lonny exclaimed and kissed her soundly.

Slaying Dragons

[Cara struggles to take care of herself and her son on a pittance while attending college. Perry, another non-traditional student, sees her walking to school in the bitter cold and offers her a ride. Cara soon discovers he has much more to offer than that.]

"Come *on*, Sammy, we have to leave *now*, or you'll be late for daycare, and Mommy will be late for college!"

"Okay, Mommy, I'm ready." Sammy pulled his knit hat on, grabbed his little backpack and followed Cara out the door, reaching for her gloved hand with his mittened one as they clambered down the stairs to the slushy streets below.

It was bitterly cold, but Sammy didn't complain as they walked the mile to Loving Arms, his preschool, not even when Cara made him stumble in her rush to get them both to school on time. He was the sweetest little boy, good-natured, kind, and loving. Cara wished she didn't have to drag him out in this weather; wished she had a car; wished for a lot of things...

No matter. What mattered was finishing her degree in Early Childhood Education so she could become a teacher and provide a better life for them both.

When they were rounding the corner of the street that Loving Arms was on, Sammy asked, "Wanna sing the Balentine song, Mommy?"

"Sure sweetie, you first," Cara replied, smiling down into Sammy's bright blue eyes.

"Cream, cream, Caraline! Won't you be my Balentine?" Sammy beseeched.

"No, no, not this time, I won't be your Valentine," Cara retorted.

"I'll slay a dragon, an' hang him on the line, if you be my Balentine," Sammy promised.

"Go slay a dragon, and hang him on the line, but I won't be your Valentine!" Cara sang then stopped abruptly. "Oh, sweetie, we're here, now. We'll sing the rest later."

"But you'll really be my Balentine, won't you Mommy, I mean, Cream Caraline?"

"Of course, Mommy—I mean, Queen Caraline—will always be your Valentine, honey. I love you *so* much," Cara replied as she bent down to give him a big squeezy hug. "Be a good boy today, and have fun! I'll see you when I'm done."

Cara sighed as she left the warmth of the cheery little school—another mile and a half to walk to reach the college. Sammy, thank goodness, was too young to realize they were so poor there wasn't money for bus fare. He thought it was fun to go to the soup kitchen for dinner and eat with the homeless people every day. At least they weren't homeless, too. They had a roof over their heads, even if it was only a dumpy little one-bedroom apartment in a rundown building.

She trudged on through the slush, head down, engrossed in her thoughts, which centered mainly on past mistakes, when a car pulled up alongside her.

"Hello!" a man's voice called. "Need a ride?"

Without looking up, she replied automatically, "No thanks, I can walk."

"But wouldn't you rather have a ride out to the college?"

That got her attention. Head still down, she asked suspiciously, "How do you know I attend college?"

"Because I'm in your Child Development class, and I see you every day—even though you've apparently never noticed me." His tone was wounded.

At that, Cara's head snapped up, and she found herself looking into the face she dreamed about alone in her bed at night. "Perry?" she asked, feeling foolish.

"The one and only, at least in this neighborhood. Now why don't you hop in and let me drive you the last mile? I'll even be a really nice guy and bring you home again."

"But I don't go right home; I have to pick up my son from daycare," Cara blurted then wished she could take it back. Why was she always so honest? Now he wouldn't want another thing to do with her. Single men didn't like being saddled with an "instant" family.

"You mean you *walk* your little boy to daycare then *walk* to school in this mess?"

Cara nodded, too ashamed to speak. Now Perry knew how destitute they were. He wouldn't offer her a ride again.

"Well, that's gonna stop right now!" he growled. "Bad enough *you* brave the elements, let alone your little guy. I'll take both of you both ways from now on."

"That's not your responsibility," Cara protested.

"I'm making it my responsibility," Perry said sternly, but his hazel eyes twinkled. "Besides, I'm already going your way, so what's a little jog over to the preschool to drop off and pick up your son?"

"I don't know how to thank you."

"I'm sure we'll think of something." Perry waggled his eyebrows up and down.

Cara giggled.

"That's better," he grinned. "I like making you smile."

They met in the commons for lunch. Over the pizza and cokes Perry bought, Cara told him how she'd quit high school to run off with a bad boy who'd dumped her as soon as she told him she was pregnant; how she struggled to raise Sammy on the pittance they got from Family Assistance; how determined she was to provide a better life for Sammy than the one he'd had so far.

"I admire you for that." Perry wiped pizza sauce off his neatly trimmed beard. "If there's anything more I can do to help, just let me know."

As they chatted, Cara discovered the reason Perry was also a non-traditional student. It was because he'd been in the military and was now attending on the G.I. Bill. He'd never been stationed outside the US, for which he was grateful, since he didn't endorse war.

Cara told him, "There are more battles being fought on home territory than you realize."

He understood right away that she referred to gang wars and was gun shy, in more ways than one.

Wisely, Perry didn't offer to be anything more than a friend to her and Sammy. Over the next week, he not only chauffeured them to and from school, he took them to dinner on Wednesday and to the college basketball game on Friday.

During half-time, Cara and Perry discussed their upcoming Child Development observation. "It'll be interesting to see how our kids are being sexually programmed," Perry commented.

"Yeah. Sammy's coming with me on Monday, aren't you Sammy?"

"Huh?" Sammy asked, busy chowing down a hot dog.

"Nothing, sweetie."

"Since we each need a three or four-year-old subject, I'm bringing my niece. I hope she doesn't embarrass me." Perry grinned.

"Well, as they say, 'out of the mouths of babes'. Watch out, or she might give away your secrets."

After the game, Perry dropped them off, and Cara put Sammy to bed. Then she looked at her calendar and sighed. Valentine's Day was next Tuesday, and she had to cough up Valentines for Sammy's classmates. They'd just have to make them with whatever she could find around the apartment. She sighed again. She didn't mind making Valentines with Sammy—it wasn't that. Valentine's Day was always hard for her. That was the day Roger had left her. The fifth anniversary of being single and alone was in five more days, and being too broke to purchase ready-made Valentines didn't help.

On Monday, groups of Child Development students were ready to give the little ones "assignments" and ask them questions to determine sexual stereotyping.

One group set out "boy" toys and "girl" toys and watched which ones the children gravitated to. Cara was proud when Sammy picked up a doll and bottle and proceeded to "feed the baby", then reached into his pocket to give his own Matchbox™ truck to a little girl who cried when another boy wrenched a car out of her hands.

A second group had constructed a cardboard house in one corner of the room, and they watched how the kids played in it. Sammy helped do dishes and cook. At this, Perry caught Cara's eye and winked.

Soon, it was Sammy's turn to be interviewed by Perry's group. One young woman asked, "Is it okay for girls to work?"

Sammy said, "Yes, it's okay. My mommy works very hard going to college and taking care of me."

Another student asked, "Is it okay for boys to cry?"

Sammy said, "Yep. Mommy says I should cry when I need to so the tears don't get stuck and come out mean things, like hitting. I cry when my feelings hurt, or when I get a boo-boo, or when I'm sad."

At that, all the students in the room stopped to listen to what Sammy would say next.

"Is it okay for a boy to tell someone that they love

them?" Perry asked Sammy, his glance at Cara indecipherable.

"Yep! And I want to tell somebody right now, okay?" He looked to Perry for permission.

"Sure, Sammy. Go right ahead."

Sammy ran to Cara and threw his arms around her. "I love you, Mommy!"

"Aww!" the other students and the professor chorused. Cara wiped tears from her face as she hugged her precious boy and told him she loved him, too.

After the other students departed with their borrowed children and the room had been restored to order, Perry's sister picked up his niece, and Cara and Sammy walked with Perry to his car.

"We'd better buy that boy an ice-cream cone; he made you look terrific!" Perry chortled.

"He made me *feel* terrific, and he's my sweet little Valentine, aren't you Sammy?"

"Yep, 'cause I slayed the dragon!"

"What?" Perry asked. Obviously, he hadn't heard the "Queen Caroline" aka "Cream Caraline" song.

"Not important. What's important is that my little man here is the only Valentine I need."

"I wouldn't be so sure of that," Perry responded, a world of meaning in his tone. "Sammy, what's this about dragons?" he asked, taking each of them by the hand. "I think I need to slay one, too."

Cara smiled and inwardly hugged herself. Perry wanted to "slay dragons" for her. It was going to be a very happy Valentine's Day; she was now one hundred percent certain of that.

Bodacious Flirtatious

[Officer Cliff Turner is about to slap the cuffs on a speeder who brazenly attempts to flirt with him in order to get out of a ticket, but after discovering the true reason Jeralyn was speeding, he has a change of heart.]

Officer Cliff Turner flipped the switch for his siren. The car in front of him was doing 65 in a 40-mile zone. Ticket time!

When the vehicle finally came to a stop on the berm of the road, he approached with caution. Drivers as reckless as this one could be dangerous.

The driver's side window came down, and out popped a head of riotous red curls. Huge, sea green eyes stared up at him in feigned innocence. "Something wrong, Officer?"

"Driver's license and registration, please." His tone was gruff.

The woman leaned over and opened her glove compartment, then her purse, displaying feminine curves. She handed him the items, her fingers brushing against his. "Anything for you, handsome." She slanted him a look that could have melted metal.

Ignoring the jolt of electricity that flashed through him at her touch, and the heat in her gaze, Cliff told her, "You were speeding in excess of 20 miles over the limit. Stay put while I run these."

"Hurry back, sugar," she said in a sultry voice.

Cliff shook his head as he walked away. The woman was nuts. If he "hurried back" it would be to give her the ticket she so richly deserved. Did she really think flirting with him would get her out of it? And what if, besides being an officer of the law, he was married? Had she no shame? If she kept up the inappropriate flirting, he'd find other infractions to add to the ticket.

When he walked back to her sporty, low-slung, screaming red Corvette with ticket pad in hand, Jeralyn Jeffers' luscious Cupid's bow mouth pouted up at him. "Please, Officer..." she paused, obviously expecting him to fill in the blank.

"Turner," he supplied tersely.

"Turner," she repeated. "Last name, right? What's your first name, hottie?" She batted curly red-brown eyelashes at him.

"Miss Jeffers, this isn't a meet and greet. You're about to get a ticket with a whopping fine attached."

"You know both my names; it's only fair I know yours," she replied, undeterred.

Irritation mixed with grudging admiration for her nerve welled in him. "It's Cliff, okay? But just because I shared privileged information with you doesn't mean I'll let you out of this." He started writing the ticket.

"Cliff, sweetheart, please stop!" Jeralyn cried. "You don't understand!" Her coy act fell away, and when he saw her crestfallen expression, he felt compelled to listen.

"What don't I understand?" His pen halted.

"I...I'm late...for a very important appointment," she stammered, looking sheepish.

"That's the usual reason for speeding." Cliff was unmoved. "You should have allowed more time to get to wherever it was you were going."

"Yes, I know, but I misplaced my car keys and spent an extra hour trying to find them. I've got to get to my finals, or my whole life from here on will go down the drain. Please...I'm the first person in my family to even have the chance to graduate college. I'm scared to death as it is. Please, forget the ticket and help me!"

Cliff shut the cover on his ticket book. "Alright, you win. Tell me where to go and stay behind me."

He got in his cruiser and turned his siren on to lead the way to the university Jeralyn named. Once at the campus, he watched her walk into the psychology building. Had she been playing some sort of head game with him, doing some sort of psychological experiment by flirting with him? Unfortunately, he didn't have time to stew about it. He had to get back on patrol.

But, for the rest of the day, Cliff couldn't get Jeralyn out of his mind. He wondered if she'd passed her exams. He wondered how she would take it if she failed. Her blue-green eyes and flame-red curls haunted him. The memory of her bodacious, outrageous flirting still stirred him up, although it shouldn't have; he'd been trained to remain detached.

Then, he did something that could cost him his badge. He tore the ticket with her personal information on it out of his book and slipped it into his pocket. When his shift was over, he drove to her house.

"Cliff!" Jeralyn exclaimed, as she opened the door to his knock.

"Hi, Jeralyn." He cleared his throat, suddenly uncomfortable. "I came to see how things went with your exams today."

"I was horribly nervous, but I think I passed."

"That's terrific. Goodnight then." Cliff forced himself to turn away.

"Don't go, hot stuff." The flirt was back.

Cliff pivoted and narrowed his eyes. "Why are you flirting with me again? And why did you waste time flirting with me this morning, if you were so late? Was I some sort of test to you, too?" he frowned.

Jeralyn's lashes fluttered downward as a rosy pink flush stained her cheeks. "No. I'm sorry, I don't normally flirt, but when I see you, I can't seem to help myself."

Cliff couldn't help himself, either. He leaned in and kissed her. Jeralyn, with her crazy red curls and outrageous suggestiveness, was just the ticket for him.

Taken Out of Con-TEXT

[Carey receives some messages on her cell phone that are clearly meant for someone else. She texts the sender that he has the wrong person, but he doesn't reply, so she goes to the meeting place he suggests to set him straight.]

[Author's note: The texting in this story is antiquated, I know, but I wrote the first draft years ago, and I think it's still great just the way it is. I hope you, dear Reader, agree!]

Carey's cell phone pinged once—incoming text. Strange, she'd informed all her friends that she preferred live calls. Who could it be? When she opened the text, the number wasn't one she recognized. "cu 2nite?" it read.

Even though she didn't like texting, she did know the language—somewhat. "diku?" *Do I know you?* she texted back.

A full minute later, the response finally came. "Aw, honey, pls db (*don't be*) mad. Simone's @ 8. Ily. (*I love you.*)"

"idku!" (*I don't know you!*) Carey texted frantically. There was no reply. She dialed the associated number. Nothing. The sender must've turned his cell off, refusing to take no for an answer. Well then, it was his tough luck if he got stood up. He probably deserved it, anyway, judging from the "pls db mad" text he'd sent.

But, as the day wore on, Carey couldn't help feeling guilty. Even though it wasn't her fault, this man believed he'd reached someone else. If "honey" didn't show up, it could cause further problems in what seemed to be an already troubled relationship.

By 7:00 that evening, Carey's mind was made up. She drove to Simone's, a popular French restaurant a half hour outside the town limits, then sat in her car in the parking lot as the digits on the dashboard clock drew closer and closer to 8:00.

Okay, smarty, she reprimanded herself. *Now what? You drove all the way out here to talk to this guy when you don't even know his name or what he looks like.* She pulled her cell out, hoping he'd finally replied to her last text.

Then the lightbulb came on. Duh! She'd wasted her gas coming here. Feeling foolish, she dialed his number.

"Hello, who is this?" a vaguely familiar, pleasant-sounding baritone voice answered. He obviously hadn't recognized her number.

"Um, it's the person you texted this morning. I don't know who you were trying to reach, but you didn't reach her."

"What?! Why didn't you call back and let me know?" His tone was distressed.

"I tried to, several times, actually. Your phone must have been off."

"Oh-h-h no!" he groaned. "I do that sometimes—hold the END button down too long. I don't even realize I've done it until something like this happens." Carey heard him heave a deep sigh. "Well, thanks for letting me know."

"You're welcome." Carey hung up and drove away, somehow feeling jealous of a woman she hadn't even met, a woman who had a man with a great voice and enough money to treat her to the best restaurant around.

Back at home, Carey pulled a microwavable dinner from the freezer, nuked it and ate it with distaste. Why was she still hung up on the situation? Why couldn't she accept that a life such as the one she pictured the woman had wasn't for her and move on? Because she'd once been *this* close to it, that's why. She'd once had a great guy like that, but she was so into work that he let her go.

Carey watched one of her romantic comedy DVD's with ill-humor and went to bed, alone and dissatisfied.

The next morning, her cell phone pinged again. What was it with all these texts all of a sudden?

She looked at the number associated with this latest one, astounded. Surely, he realized by now this wasn't his girlfriend's number?

"ht (*hey there*), hay (*how are you*) 2day?"

"pls call me, I don't like 2 text," she typed and hung up.

A few seconds later, her cell rang. Yep, it was him, calling her as asked. A smile lit her face, but then she sobered. What was she doing, getting all excited because an attached man was calling her? What was wrong with her?

"What do you want?" she snapped more out of anger at herself for being so amoral than anything else.

"Whoa there... I only wanted to thank you again, not that it did me any good. I still got stood up."

"Whatever problems you and your girlfriend are having, leave me out of them, okay?" Carey snarled.

"Well, you see, that's the thing, I don't have a girlfriend anymore, but I wondered..." he cleared his throat "if I could take *you* to Simone's tonight to thank you."

"Wow, talk about the world's fastest rebound! You're something else, you know that? I don't know a thing about you—except that you rush into—and apparently out of—things too fast."

Two beats of silence followed. Then he said, "You're right about one thing. You don't know me, as you texted yesterday. You've judged me wrongly, taken a few words completely out of context. But how are you ever going to discover what's true about me unless you take me up on my offer?"

"Fine. Simone's at 8:00?"

"Simone's at 8:00," he confirmed, a smile in his voice.

"How will I know you? How will you know me?"

"Oh, I'll know you, pretty lady with the dark hair and eyes," he replied and hung up.

Flabbergasted, Carey nonetheless showed up at 8:00.

In the lobby of Simone's he waited, his sandy brown hair and dark chocolate eyes a dead giveaway. It was her ex-fiancé, the one she had thought to be completely out of the context of her life.

"You were right about one thing," Jeff said as he put his hand at her waist to guide her to the table he'd reserved. "I did rush out of things too fast. I still love you."

Carey smiled inwardly as she thought, but didn't say just yet, *ily2 (I love you, too).*

The Condensed Version

[A "luck of the Irish" fast-paced, "love at first sight" tale, starring Sersha and Brendan.]

This band is really good, Sersha thought as she danced energetically with her girlfriends. Abruptly, the song they were dancing to ended before it was supposed to.

Coming to a stop, Sersha glanced up at the musicians on the stage and saw them shrugging in confusion. Then the cute guy playing the Epiphone electric guitar chuckled a bit sheepishly and said, "Sorry folks, you just got the condensed version. We'll have to play the long version for you next time."

She already knew Cute Guy had a fantastic singing voice because the "condensed song" was "Love Somebody Like You" by Keith Urban, and Cute Guy had been killing it when someone in the band faltered. Now that Sersha had discovered he also had the most swoon worthy speaking voice, it made her want to follow him wherever he went, as if he were the Pied Piper.

When Cute Guy announced at the end of their final set that they would be playing at the Electric Techno Lounge the following weekend, Sersha told her friends, "I'm going!"

She had no idea whether he was single or married, or if he had a girlfriend. Most likely, he was unattached because the girlfriends and wives of musicians usually danced in a group while their men played, but tonight there'd been no such group in sight. Sersha sure hoped she was right about that because she was already halfway in love with him.

Cute Guy, aka Brendan, set his Epiphone on its stand and jumped down off the stage immediately after the last set ended, anxious to catch up with the cute girl he'd seen dancing with her friends. Usually, he didn't try to hook up with anybody after a show like his buddies did. But tonight, he had barely been able to keep his mind on his music because he'd been so mesmerized by her flaming hair flying in all directions as she pranced around the floor on shapely legs. (He was the culprit who'd missed a chord and caused the song to crash earlier.)

Sprinting, Brendan managed to catch up to her just in time to hold the door open as she exited The Dry Dock, the bar where they'd been playing.

Surprised, Sersha said, "Oh, thank you..." and let her voice trail off, waiting for Cute Guy to supply his name.

"Brendan," he said, "and what's your name, Cute Girl?"

"Sersha," she answered with a smug smile. So, Brendan thought she was "cute", too. This had to be a sign, a good luck sign! And Sersha, being Irish, very much believed in luck, especially with Saint Paddy's day just around the corner.

When they were both standing on the sidewalk outside, Brendan asked Sersha, "Would you mind coming back inside with me while I help break down the set? After that, I'd be happy to take you to breakfast. There's an all-night diner not too far from here."

Sersha couldn't believe her amazing luck. She had already snagged a first date! "Sure," she said. "Anything I can do to help?"

"No, you just sit pretty while I help the guys. Would you like another drink while you wait?"

"I'll have a cherry coke, thanks."

So, Sersha doesn't drink, either, and she's partial to cherry cokes, Brendan thought. *Two things in common already. It has to be a sign, a good sign!*

At the diner, the couple ate their way through Everything breakfasts (eggs, bacon, sausage, hash browns, and pancakes) and drank multiple cups of coffee while they talked the night away discovering they had much in common, but not too much. Both could tell they had the makings of a number one hit song together. Neither of them was inclined to go home as the dawn broke.

Since it was Sunday, they spent the whole day together. After they plundered the local grocery store for ready-made sandwiches, cheese, crackers, and other munchables, bottled water and cherry cokes, Brendan took her to see some mini waterfalls that Sersha hadn't even realized were there, and he had only been in town for a couple of months while she'd been born here.

They spread a blanket in the shade along the shore of the river and had a picnic, a day long picnic. As the sun began to set, they were once again loathe to leave each other, but both had to prepare for the workweek ahead.

At her door, Brendan gave Sersha a chaste kiss, but she could feel the restrained heat behind it. "Catch you later," he said in an offhand way, trying to downplay his reluctance to leave her.

"If you're lucky," Sersha teased, her eyes filled with mischief.

Brendan, his own eyes glimmering with devilry, said, "You little scamp! Now, you leave me no choice. I'll just have to prove to you how lucky I am!" Then he pulled her close and gave her a winning kiss.

And Sersha had no choice but to concede that Brendan was a champion kisser, and he'd just won her heart, too, although she wasn't about to tell him that. "Okay, okay! You're lucky!" she laughingly agreed. "See you tomorrow?"

"If—"

"And don't you dare say, 'If you're lucky'!"

During the rest of the week that followed, the couple found time every day to spend with each other, even though they both worked full-time jobs in the technology sector—Sersha as a website designer and Brendan as a mobile app developer. And every hour that they spent together brought them closer and closer, but not too close.

Sersha, despite her modern job, and her forward thinking, was actually an old-fashioned girl at heart, which meant she wasn't willing to give anyone anything more than her heart without a commitment, and Brendan respected that. He more than respected that, he agreed with it, surprising himself when he realized he was already more than happy to make a long-term commitment to Sersha.

Saturday, which just happened to be St. Patrick's Day, Brendan and the band, re-named Lucky Dogs just for the night, played together at the Electric Techno Lounge, and he dedicated "On Top of the World" by the Imagine Dragons to Sersha.

Their one-week anniversary was Sunday, and they spent it together, strolling through the park on the shore of Lake Erie, sailing in a small dinghy, laughing, teasing each other, and just having the best time.

Back on land, Sersha loved Brendan's wicked smile as he told her, tongue in cheek, "I once caught a walleye as big as a person."

"No you didn't!" Sersha laughed.

"You're right, I didn't, but I did catch *you*!" he said as he scooped her up off the sand and swung her around.

Sersha squealed and said, "Put me down!"

Brendan replied, "Only if you say the magic words."

"And what would those words be?" Sersha asked.

"I'll give you a hint. There are three words, and the first word is I."

"I want down!" Sersha teased.

"Nope, not it!"

"I like you."

"Getting warmer, but still not it." By this point, Brendan was holding Sersha in his arms like she was a baby, and he gazed down at her with loving eyes. "How about I say them first?" he asked.

Is he about to say what I think he is, already? Sersha's heart pounded in anticipation.

"I love you," Brendan said softly.

"Wow! That's fast!"

"I know, it's the condensed version," Brendan said and kissed her breathless.

When they finally came up for air, Sersha said, "I love you, too, and I love the condensed version."

Brendan kissed her again and said, "Just wait until we get to the long version."

"Oh, I'm so lucky!" Sersha exclaimed.

"Not any luckier than I am!" Brendan replied. "We both get to spend a lifetime together."

Party Girl

[Poppy plans a pirate party for a seven-year-old whose father seems to be a Blackbeard because he keeps hitting on her. Attracted, but determined not to become the spoils of one of his illicit raids, Poppy is prepared to tell her client, the child's mother, about his unwanted advances when she is robbed of all her protests.]

Poppy drove up the circular drive to the mansion, nerve ends zinging. It was crucial that she get this new client, or Poppy's Perfect Parties would go under.

"Oh, I'm so glad you found us!" the woman she'd spoken to on the phone earlier exclaimed, gazing at the logo plastered on the side of Poppy's Smart car. "I'm Anne. Come on in. I hope your service can provide the party we're looking for."

"I hope so, too," Poppy murmured. "I brought some samples of parties I've done in the past."

Anne flipped through photos of movie-themed children's parties in the binder Poppy handed her after they were both seated. "These are fantastic! Have you ever done one with pirates? Eddie's favorite movie is *The Pirates: Band of Misfits*. He loves that fat parrot."

"No, no pirates, but I'm sure I can come up with some ideas."

"Great! Think you can do that by two o'clock this afternoon? I want to keep this a complete secret from Eddie, and he gets home from school around 3:20."

"No problem." Poppy put on her brainstorming hat and began to sketch out some rough ideas. "How about... a pirate's ship with portholes made from discarded refrigerator boxes that the kids can crawl through... skull and crossbones sails made from old sheets... scavenger treasure hunt complete with maps... pin the eye patch on the pirate... parrot piñata... goodie bags filled with chocolate gold doubloons, spyglasses, eye patches..."

"Stop! No, don't stop. You're hired. The party is in two weeks, though. Can you pull everything together that fast?"

Poppy didn't tell Anne that she had no other clients at the moment. "I'm sure I can squeeze it in."

* * *

During school days over the next two weeks, Poppy put her creativity to work, and Anne helped. They were painting brown boards on the sides of the refrigerator box "pirate ship" when a man who could've been a buccaneer himself with his dark good looks strolled into the garage where they were set up. He gave Anne a resounding kiss on the cheek accompanied by a big, squeezy hug. "How's my best girl today?" he asked and Poppy, who'd felt an instant surge of attraction toward him, squelched it. *This must be Eddie's father; Eddie looks just like him.*

Anne introduced Poppy to Abe and explained that they were concocting the party here in the garage and keeping it locked so Eddie wouldn't see.

"Good idea," Abe said. "It all looks great. And such a pretty party girl you hired, Anne," he added, eyeing Poppy in a way that wasn't kosher for a married man. Poppy squirmed inwardly and hoped he wasn't one of those nasty, groping, two-timer hubbies. Such a shame. Anne was beautiful and super nice. She didn't deserve a guy like that.

The next day, Poppy was painting skulls and crossbones on the pirate ship's sails while Anne ran an errand, when in walked Abe. "Hey, there, pretty party girl, wanna come party with me sometime?" he asked and flashed her a wicked smile.

Cheater! Poppy looked away and made no outward response, even though inwardly her timbers shivered traitorously.

"What's the matter?" Abe asked in mock confusion. "Did I say or do something wrong?"

You know what you said. You know what you're doing—or trying to do—Blackbeard, but it ain't gonna happen with me. Poppy shook her head wordlessly, feeling skewered. If she upset him, he might fire her. Better tread lightly on that plank lest she drown.

Just then Anne returned, so Poppy was spared any further need to speak to the louse.

But Blackbeard wasn't about to be deflected so easily. Nearly every day, he popped in at lunchtime to check on Poppy's progress—and to whisper suggestively in her ear when Anne wasn't around. Unfortunately for Poppy, Anne always seemed to have some chore or errand to attend to right around noon. *How strange that Anne never seems to want to be here when her husband comes home for lunch,* Poppy thought, as she dodged unwanted advance after unwanted advance from Abe.

(Or at least she was doing her best to tell herself she didn't like Abe's attentions. But her treacherous body wasn't listening to her, and it was getting harder and harder to resist him.)

* * *

Eddie's seventh birthday arrived, and Poppy told herself that she was relieved. She had sent out homemade invitations the first day on the job with the words, "Captain Eddie invites you to an 'award-winning' party" above a picture of the pirates from the movie on the front. Apparently, they were a hit. All thirty children, Eddie's entire second grade class, and their parents, came.

But the birthday boy's father was conspicuously absent. Where was he? It was Sunday afternoon, so surely he wasn't working. Poppy tried to convince herself that she was simply concerned for the boy and his mother. She did not—repeat—DID NOT care whether the rogue showed up on her account.

The celebration was in full swing, and the kids were scrambling to find the scavenger hunt "treasures" hidden around the backyard when Abe finally arrived, the scoundrel. Poppy allowed herself to scowl at him. He couldn't fire her now. The party was a done deal.

Eddie's face lit up, and he raced toward the reprobate yelling, "Uncle Abe! Uncle Abe!"

Uncle? Abe is Eddie's uncle? Mental head slap!

"Hello, bro," Anne called to him, confirming the fact.

This time, when Abe flashed her that rakish plunderer's smile, Poppy flashed it back. *Ahoy, matey! I'll sail off into the sunset with you anytime. Let's get this party started!*

Stealing His Heart

[Zona resorts to her old habit of pickpocketing in an attempt to find a suitable suitor, only to discover her target is off-duty policeman, Otto Owens.]

Zona had been at it every morning for the past month with no luck. If she didn't succeed soon, she'd have to acknowledge that this was the craziest scheme ever and give up.

"Thanks, Dad," she said rolling her eyes heavenward. "Thanks ever so much for your guidance." Sarcasm laced her voice as she recalled the man who had made her assist him in his thievery from toddlerhood. They'd been busted together when she was barely a teen for hustling in downtown Chicago, and she'd been taken away from him. Zona hadn't seen him again.

Ever since his funeral, nutty ideas that she could only assume came from her father kept popping into her head. Like this latest—*Steal their wallets, that way you can find out if they're married, dating or single. Then you can give the wallets back—oops, you dropped this—and maybe some poor schmuck will believe you and be grateful long enough for you to get your hooks into him. At your age, darlin', beggars can't be choosers. You gotta do something to get a man before it's too late.*

Zona didn't know why she was going along with it, but she studied the men trying to beat the clock as they strode along the sidewalk in downtown Nashville and sighed. They looked too old, too stodgy. Most likely married, every one of them. These guys didn't even merit picking their pockets, or running the risk of getting caught.

This was a new venue for Zona in a brand new city. She'd thought she might meet someone interesting on Demonbreun Street because it was so close to the Country Music Hall of Fame—perhaps a singer, a songwriter, an agent, or a producer. But, apparently they weren't around in the daylight, and it was too risky to try to pull this off at night. She'd hang out here for five more minutes and leave.

Then she saw him.

From the moment Zona laid eyes on his slim but muscular physique, his sun-kissed gold-brown hair, his twinkling blue eyes that seemed out of place among all the lackluster orbs around him, and his sensuous mouth bracketed by the most adorable dimples, she knew she had to make a play for him. If he turned out to be married, she'd just die.

Zona watched with bated breath as he drew closer and closer, as he finally noticed her and flashed her a smile that cinched things. That smile was as sexy as his lips, and the heat of it sent a thrill through her.

Finally, he was abreast of her. "Hi there," he said in a voice like molten honey.

"Hi," she said breathlessly, deliberately faking an awkward stumble, grabbing him around the waist for balance and deftly removing the desired item from his back pocket.

"Sorry," Zona said, straightening and thrusting the hand that held his wallet behind her back. "Your smile threw me off balance."

"I'm sorry, too," he said, taking her firmly by the arm, "but you're coming with me to the police station. Pick-pocketing is a serious offense in this city." He grabbed his wallet out of her hand with his free one and put it in his front pants pocket.

She didn't struggle as he marched her around the corner and down the block. *I knew better than to listen to you, Dad. Now, I'll have an adult record, one that can't be expunged.*

In minutes, they were at the front doors of the Central Police Precinct. *Wonderful,* she thought, *I had to pick a place right by the station.*

"Stop, *please!*" she urged. "May I ask you to listen to

me for just a minute before you take me inside?"

The eyes that had been so warm moments ago were now ice-blue shards that stabbed into hers. "Fine, but don't think your sob story's going to change anything."

"Would you mind if I took a look inside your wallet?"

"Are you nuts?" his face flushed with anger.

"Certifiably, but I need to see what's in there, please."

"Why do you want to see what's in my wallet? Are your sticky little fingers itching?"

"No. I wasn't going to steal anything from you, honest. I was only going to take a peek and give it back."

"Oh, so now you want me to believe you're just some weird voyeur who gets her kicks from looking at other people's pictures and stuff? That you're not out to steal my money or credit cards or identity?" His tone was incredulous.

"What use would I have for a man's credit cards or his identity?" she asked, desperate to make him see she was telling the truth.

"Maybe you're not working alone. Maybe you have a male partner in crime."

"I wish I had a male partner!" she cried, throwing up her hands. "That's what I wanted to see. Whether or not you were single." She lowered her head and her voice trailed off.

"And I thought I'd heard it all," he muttered in disgust, pushing open the glass door and dragging her into the lobby of the station with him.

"'Lo, Officer Owens, what have you got now?"

Her head jerked up and her eyes flew to his. "You're a policeman?"

"All day, every day. Oliver Owens, at your service."

"This can't be happening. It just can't," she shook her head not realizing she spoke aloud.

"Oh, trust me it is," he said in a low voice. In a louder one, he replied to the desk clerk, "I've got a common little thief. She just tried to lift my wallet."

"That's rich!" The clerk threw back his head and guffawed. "She must be the dumbest pickpocket on earth. Either that or she's from another planet."

"I'm new in town," Zona muttered, embarrassed.

After she was Miranda-ed, fingerprinted, and booked, the booking agent led her to a pod. She plunked down on a bench to await arraignment and her fate.

But fate surprised her. Later in the day, the pod door slid open and she was free to go. As she walked to Receiving to collect her things, a familiar voice spoke from behind her. "I couldn't find any record on you, so I took a chance you were telling me the truth, wacko as it seemed, and I sprang you. How about returning the favor and having dinner with me?"

Zona whirled around. Doubt and disbelief warred with the joy on her face, but joy won out as she saw by the solemnity of his eyes that he was serious. "Yes," she toned the whoop that rose in her throat down to a whisper and answered, "Yes."

Fool Me, April

[Randy, who has loved April since they were kids, puts up with all her pranks just to keep her in his life, so he's flabbergasted when April shows him she's serious.]

Randy couldn't help it, he was still head over heels in love with April, even though she was constantly pranking him. She'd been tricking him since they were kids. She colored unboiled eggs one Easter then dared him to crack one on his head, made a birthday card that said it had a ten dollar bill inside but wouldn't open, told a girl he liked her when he didn't on Valentine's Day, and gave him an empty box within a box, within a box, within a box, as a present at Christmas. But it wasn't just holidays—to April, every day presented a new opportunity to get his goat.

Once, she swiped his clothes when he was skinny dipping with some of the guys. Another time, she told him to follow her and led him right into a bog, which sucked him in up to his waist. As they grew older, April resorted to things like making him muffins that were salty instead of sweet, snarling up his remote so he couldn't watch his beloved football games, and on and on, ad nauseam.

When April finally ran out of ideas, she actually bought a baby goat and brought it to his office on the first working day of the new year. She informed him, "This pet's a reminder that I won't try to get your goat anymore."

But Randy didn't trust that for a minute; he was still stuck with a farm animal and no place to raise it. He'd had to ask a local farmer to adopt the baby goat. No "kidding". Having April as a friend (and wanting more) wasn't punny.

April hadn't played any jokes on him in months, not since the baby goat, but April Fool's Day, her most favorite holiday of all, was coming up. Randy was on red alert. He knew she wouldn't be able to resist doing something to him on that day of all days.

But as of the first evening in April, no joke had been played. All Randy had received from his friend was a dumb card that read: "Knock, knock! *Who's there?* Noah. *Noah who?* Noah good April Fools' joke?" Below the punchline inside the card, April had written: Seriously, I'm all out. Would you please come to dinner at my place tonight? No fooling, no pranking, just a nice meal. Your pal, April.

Okay, Randy, he told himself, *get ready. April Fool's Day isn't over yet. April has just been storing up her pranks.*

As he knocked on her door, Randy steeled himself to become the target of the mother of all April Fool's jokes.

Yet, when April answered his knock, the only thing she said was, "What, no dumb knock-knock joke as a comeback?"

Nothing fell on his head, nothing jumped out at him, nothing...

Randy put his hand on her forehead and asked, "Are you sick, April?"

She swatted his hand away lightly and said, "Very funny. I promised you when I gave you the baby goat that I wouldn't try to get *your goat* anymore, and I haven't. I even wrote in the card that I was all out of jokes, and I meant it."

"Yeah, right, April. You forget I know you all too well. What did you make for dinner, hmm?" Randy headed for her kitchen, ready to make a thorough inspection. Maybe there was a ghost pepper added to a pot of chili, or something inedible hidden in a salad. He still hadn't forgotten the sponge cake she'd made for his birthday a few years back.

It was a large sheet cake with beautifully decorated cream cheese frosting—Randy's favorite. April had already cut him the first piece and handed it to him. But he couldn't get his fork through the cake. Forgetting her penchant for pulling pranks, he said, "Geez, April, this cake is way too dry! I can't even get a bite on my fork. What did you make it with?"

April had burst into gales of laughter. It took her a full minute to calm down before she answered, "It's a *sponge* cake, so what do you think I used—a real sponge!" Then she went into another laughing fit.

However, dinner tonight was perfect. April had prepared his favorite Ranch dressing roasted chicken, mashed potatoes with gravy made from the drippings, and steamed asparagus. Dessert was strawberry shortcake, another favorite, and there wasn't even shaving cream instead of whipped cream on top. What was up with her?

After she cleared the table and brought their drinks into the living room, they sat side by side on the sofa in front of her gas fireplace.

He cleared his throat and said, "Dinner was great, but seriously, April, what's wrong? You've never let an April Fool's Day slide by without tricking me in some way before."

"'Seriously' is the operative word here, Randy. It's high time I stopped joking around."

"Wha—?"

April covered his mouth with hers. They kissed for what seemed like hours before coming up for air. When they did, she told her flummoxed friend, "I've loved you for years, ever since we were kids, but the only way I could get your attention was to prank you. Then I got stuck in the role of your jokester buddy. I kept it up because it made you laugh and want to be my friend. But I don't want to be your friend, anymore."

Randy's heart, which had been racing a second before, stopped. "You don't?"

"I want to be more than a fooling friend to you, can't you tell?"

Randy's heart started back up again as he kissed her and said, "But I like...no, love...my fooling friend. I've loved you since we were kids, too, April. That's why I let you do all the crazy stuff you did. And I've missed it these past four months, so fool me, April, whenever you want. I'll happily be your fool forever."

Marty's Heart

[Marty has a huge heart and is always helping anyone in need. He literally "gives until it hurts" when he falls off a roof while re-shingling it for a neighbor and plummets to the concrete driveway below. Then Kathy comes to his rescue and sticks around to help him through his convalescence.]

Marty Engles had a big heart, maybe too big, but then, he was a very big man. He was always helping someone someway: rescuing kittens stuck in trees, carrying groceries for the neighborhood ladies, helping their men with fix-it projects—if you asked him to do it; Marty would ensure it got done. He also volunteered at the local soup kitchen three times per week and gave generously to every representative of every worthy cause who knocked on his door.

Marty gave until it hurt.

One evening when he was nailing shingles back onto Mrs. Taylor's garage roof after a big storm hit, he lost his footing and plummeted to the concrete driveway below, breaking his right arm and his left leg in three places all totaled. Marty felt like *he* was totaled as he lay there unable to fish his cell phone out of his pants pocket and call for help. Mrs. Taylor, another do-gooder, was off attending her weekly meeting of Ladies for Change, and, since it was suppertime, no one was out and about on Paradise Street.

Groaning through gritted teeth, Marty couldn't help but fear that Mrs. Taylor wouldn't see him and would run over him when she pulled into the driveway at 8:00. He tried to wriggle his torso around so he could see the street and call for help if anyone came along before it got completely dark, but the movement shot volts of searing pain through his arm and leg, so he stopped. What was he going to do now? What *could* he do? The answer to that was a big, fat, "Nothing."

After what seemed like eons during which Marty nearly lost consciousness several times, a young woman passing by on a red bicycle braked abruptly and wheeled around to stop next to him. "Goodness!" she exclaimed. "Are you okay?" She jumped off the bicycle and knelt down next to him. "What a dumb question! Of course, you're not okay."

"Do you have a cell phone on you?" Marty croaked, his weak voice sounding unfamiliar to his ears.

"Um, no. Sorry, I don't. Maybe I can ask a neighbor to call 911."

"No need for that. I've got a cell phone in my back pocket, if you can get to it."

The woman chewed on her lower lip and gave him a dubious look. "Um, I've had first aid classes, and I don't think I should move you. Getting to your back pocket would mean rolling you on your side."

"Please, roll me over," Marty insisted. "I've been lying here suffering for about," he glanced at the angle of the setting sun, "an hour now, and I would rather endure the pain than stay like this much longer."

"You won't sue me if something goes wrong?" Her big brown eyes darkened with worry.

"Roll away. I promise to take all responsibility." Responsibility was Marty's middle name.

"O-kaay," she reluctantly agreed, positioning herself on his right side. "Take a deep breath. This is gonna hurt... No, wait... I've got to find something to immobilize your arm with first."

"There's a key under the third rock lining the sidewalk by the front door. Look inside. Mrs. Taylor has a rack of magazines." Then it struck Marty that she wouldn't have to play EMT now. "Wait a minute! Why didn't I think of this before? No need to move me and jeopardize yourself. You can just use Mrs. Taylor's home phone to call. It's on a table in the foyer as you step inside."

"Oh, great," she said, relief plain on her face. "Hang tight, I'll be right back."

When the ambulance arrived about ten minutes later, she asked the paramedics if she could go with

Marty.

"Only immediate family is allowed to ride with a patient," they informed her.

Her face fell as her eyes traveled to her bike. "Oh, okay. Good luck," she told Marty with an apologetic look on her face.

Marty knew he was going to need a lot more than "good luck". With both a broken arm and leg, he was going to be out of commission for some time to come. He had no clue how he, a bachelor, was going to manage once they sent him home from the hospital.

But, when the taxi dropped him off in his new wheelchair a couple of days later and Marty rolled himself into his house via the garage, there she was in his kitchen standing at the stove, and the most amazing aromas tantalized his nose. He didn't know how she managed it, since he only owned one pot and rarely cooked, preferring to join his friends at the soup kitchen, eat out, or nuke something in the microwave.

Stunned, Marty stammered, "W-what are you doing here and h-how did you get in?"

"I looked under all the rocks near the front door. I figured if Mrs. Taylor hid her key like that, you might, too, and I was right. I felt bad that I couldn't come and visit you in the hospital since I don't ride my bike alone after dark, and I was busy yesterday.

When I got home last evening, I asked the neighbors about you, starting with Mrs. Taylor. None of them could stop talking about what a great guy you are. They told me you were coming home today, so I decided I could afford to take a chance and help *you*, the one who's always helping others."

It turned out that she, Kathy, was between jobs, so she was available to provide him with in-home care while he convalesced. Marty was uncomfortable with the arrangement at first—he was used to being the one who gave, not received—but it wasn't long before they became good friends. When the casts came off, Marty asked Kathy out, and they became much more.

As he stood at the altar—a year to the day since his accident—and watched his beautiful bride glide toward him, Marty's big heart swelled to include Kathy forever, the woman who'd taught him that it was just as blessed to receive as it was to give.

The Right Fit

[Jessica owns an alteration shop conveniently located next to a bridal boutique. While working for a particularly unpleasant "bridezilla", she meets and secretly falls for the best man, who is in need of a lot of alteration. However, the fit is perfect in the end.]

"Shorten the hem another half-inch, will you?" the bridezilla said.

Jessica sighed inwardly. The length was ideal. If she did as asked, she'd only have to take it out again after Miss Unpleasable discovered the hem was too short. When she first opened her hole-in-the-wall alterations shop right next to the only bridal boutique in town, Jessica had been thrilled that all its customers were sent her way. Not this time.

"Take it off, and I'll see to it." Jessica stifled the huff of indignation that threatened to escape.

Bridezilla ordered, "Get it right this time," and flounced out of the store.

Jessica was tempted, childishly, to stick her tongue out at the woman behind her back.

Good thing she didn't, because just then the groom entered the shop with his best man, and boy howdy, was he ever a "best" man. Not only was he the "best" looking man Jessica had ever seen, but, he was the "best" acting one she'd ever had the pleasure of dealing with.

"Are those alterations done?" he asked, his handsome face expectant.

"Sure are, Dave!" Jessica beamed at him. "Hopefully, the suit coat will fit like a glove now. I'll just go get it and be right back."

As she walked into the storage room of Altered States, Jessica couldn't help wishing for the hundredth time that she could be more than just the alterer. The recurring daydream she'd been having ever since meeting Dave a few weeks ago—of attending the reception with him—wove its golden threads around her for a nanosecond before she shook it off and returned to the main area of the shop. No doubt Dave had a girlfriend and had already asked her to the wedding.

"Let's see if my measurements were correct this time." Jessica held the garment up by the neck so Dave could slip into it. The problem was that he was powerfully built in the chest, shoulders and arms yet didn't appear so. His torso also tapered to a very slim waist, so he'd had to purchase a large size to accommodate his bulky upper body and have it altered to fit the lower. They'd already had several alteration sessions.

As Dave buttoned the suitcoat, it was plain to see the tailoring was finally just right, and Jessica felt a pang of regret. Now, he wouldn't have any reason to come back. That was good because it meant she'd done her job, but bad because she'd miss him.

"Well, guess we're done here, then," the groom said, and settled the bill.

"Guess so," Dave agreed, sending Jessica a look she couldn't quite decipher. "Great job," he called over his shoulder as they left.

"Thanks," Jessica called back wanly.

As soon as they were gone, she hung the "Out to Lunch" sign on the door and locked up. She wasn't hungry, but she did need to rip out the seams of her ill-fitting dream. Dave was gone. He'd never be part of her life. A long walk and a good talking to herself ought to get that through her head.

The trail in front of her led to her secret place a mile away. She'd stumbled upon "her" waterfall shortly after moving to this Mother Lode community, and now, whenever she was tired, troubled or just needed a pick-me-up, she headed for the tiny clearing hidden among the pines. There, she'd sit and listen as the water tripped headlong over the cliff into the pool where she soaked her feet.

Today, the little waterfall's magic failed to soothe. Jessica mentally held the seam ripper in her hands but couldn't do it. She couldn't tear up the fabric of her dream. Instead, she allowed it to flow like silk through her mind just once more. Tipping her head back so the sun warmed her closed eyelids, Jessica saw herself, not Miss Unpleasable, walking down the aisle where Dave, not the groom, awaited. Hey, if she was going to fantasize about him for the last time, might as well go for it and admit what she really wanted.

Wriggling bare feet back and forth, Jessica enjoyed the cool, bubbling sensation of the frothy water then yelped when something bumped up against one foot. Her eyes flew open. Dave sat right beside her, feet submerged, too. He had the stealth of a mountain lion; she hadn't heard him approach, much less take off his shoes and join her.

"Hi there." His grin at her astonishment was smug. "I forgot to mention I'd like you to be my date to the wedding. Come with me?"

Jessica shook her head, sure the daydream was still in effect.

"Was that a 'no'?" His face fell like the water before them.

"No. I mean, it wasn't a 'no'. Yes, I'll go with you."

"Fantastic!" His smile outshone the sun as he moved in for a kiss, and the fit of their lips was perfect.

The Easter Basket

[A shy man with Asperger's anonymously leaves an Easter basket with a pair of one-carat diamond earrings on the front porch of the woman he's fallen for. Juliet, who is delighted but also a bit freaked out, thinks whoever left it must be a stalker because all the other items in the basket prove he knows a lot about her. When her secret admirer comes out of hiding, Juliet is astounded.]

On Good Friday, Juliet Uphill opened her front door and saw a large Easter basket sitting on the porch. "Who left this?" she wondered aloud. Pleased, but needing to get to the elementary school, Juliet took the basket inside and left it on her kitchen counter without examining it.

All day long, as she taught fourth grade, Juliet wondered about the basket. As soon as she got home, she made some tea and seated herself at the counter to open it. "Happy Easter from an admirer" was written on the attached card.

Hmm... very mysterious. Juliet untied the pink and green ribbon, and the yellow cellophane fell away. Inside was a large chocolate rabbit and a one-pound box of assorted chocolates with nuts, both from See's™. Whoever it was knew she enjoyed good chocolate. Maybe it was her friend, Nancy. She couldn't believe a man would do this.

Juliet took a sip of tea then set both items on the counter and retrieved a box of her favorite peach tea, the same kind she was drinking now, from the basket. Next, she took out some beautiful, hand-painted Easter eggs in a six-pack carton. No, it couldn't be Nancy, unless she bought them. Nancy wasn't artistic.

Curiouser and curiouser, Juliet thought, continuing to unpack the basket. Nestled in tissue was a darling ceramic bunny in a garden patch. The bunny was a lid, and the garden patch a container. Inside that was a small white box with another note that read, "Carats are my favorite thing, next to you."

Juliet gasped in awe as she opened the box to find a pair of one-carat diamond earrings. "Who *are* you?" she wondered aloud. Now it had to be a man. A woman friend might give her the ceramic bunny, but not the earrings.

The rest of the basket was filled with an assortment of small treats like Jelly Belly™ beans (her favorite), malted milk robin's eggs, marshmallow Peeps™, and non-candy items like notepads, pens, paper clips, and an "Awesome! ☺ " stamp pad.

This person knew she was a teacher, which was even more confounding because there were no male teachers at her school, and the men who did work there, like the principal and the janitor, were married.

Finished with her tea, Juliet packed everything back into the basket and retied the cellophane around it. Much as she wanted to, she couldn't keep it. Those earrings could have cost well over a thousand dollars, and she wouldn't accept such a gift unless she was engaged or married to the person. She put the basket in her pantry, a cool dry place with a door that locked, and called Nancy.

"Nancy, you won't believe what I just got!"

* * *

Liam Lamberton, a very good-looking, but extremely shy man with Aspergers, waited anxiously in the Perk You Up coffee shop for Juliet to walk through the door. She and her friend Nancy met there like clockwork every Saturday morning at nine. He sat in his usual spot, right next to their usual spot, with his coffee and his newspaper.

As soon as he saw them coming, he buried his head in the newspaper so they wouldn't notice him.

They were chattering excitedly.

"I still can't believe he actually put one-carat diamond earrings in that basket!" Nancy exclaimed. She'd gone to Juliet's the night before and had seen all that the basket held.

Whew! She got them, Liam thought.

"I *know*," Juliet replied. "It's so over-the-top, especially from some anonymous man. I can't keep them, though I would love to. I have to find him and give the basket back."

Oh no! I blew it. I just thought how nice they would look in your pretty little ears. Please, keep the basket. I want you to have it.

"*I* wouldn't give it back," Nancy said enviously.

You tell her, Nancy.

"That's just 'cause you're greedy," Juliet teased. "Seriously, it could be some whacko stalking me. I'm starting to get scared. How does this guy know so much about what I like? Or that I'm a teacher? It's spooky."

Behind his newspaper, Liam hung his head. He'd never have a chance with her now. He only wanted to make her happy. *Why do I always do the wrong thing? I won't bother you anymore*, Liam told Juliet in his mind.

* * *

Juliet awakened on Easter morning with thoughts of the basket in her head. That See's™ candy was calling her. Like a naughty little girl, she went to the pantry and unwrapped the basket, took out the box of chocolates and the chocolate bunny then wrapped it back up. *By the time I find him, these will be melted*, she rationalized.

Then she couldn't help but have a few Jelly Bellies™, robin's eggs and Peeps™. Sighing at her lack of control, Juliet decided to keep everything except for the earrings. She put the little white box containing them on a high shelf in the pantry and re-locked it. Those, she would still definitely return, if she could. Setting the cute ceramic bunny on an occasional table, Juliet thought, *I don't know who you are, but I sure do like everything you put in my basket.*

* * *

Liam spent Easter Sunday morning at church. Though he was shy, he loved to play his guitar and sing for the small congregation, and they loved to hear him. He was playing and singing when Juliet, who didn't go to church, but loved to walk in the spring sunshine, heard the music through the open doors.

It sounded so wonderful, she wandered closer and stood just outside to listen. *This guy is awesome!* she thought and poked her head around the door to see who it was. *Wow! He's as handsome as he sounds.*

Liam happened to look up at that moment, and his heart beat double-time. *It's her!* Excitement rose in his chest along with his heartbeat, but then it turned into extreme unease. *What is she doing here? Did she figure out I'm her "stalker"? Is she going to expose me to the church? I wish I'd never left her that basket.*

Juliet walked into the church and quietly found a seat in one of the back pews.

Liam got so nervous then that his beautiful baritone voice cracked, and he almost couldn't finish the song. His hands shook as he strummed the guitar, too, but he managed to finish. Thank goodness it was the end of his set for today.

The church members applauded, and leaving his guitar, Liam stepped off the raised platform to take his seat in the front row. His agitation continued to increase, despite the pastor's soothing sermon, He prayed Juliet would leave before everyone moved to the fellowship hall for the potluck to follow.

But no such luck. Just as he saw Juliet trying to duck out as quietly as she came in, Pastor Pete hurried over to invite her to stay for the festivities.

Why not? Juliet thought. *Maybe I can talk to that wonderful singer, find out if he's single.* She blushed at her instant attraction.

Liam was shocked when Juliet came to stand next to him in the buffet line. He didn't know what she'd said to Pastor Pete, but it couldn't have been bad, or Pastor would have pulled him aside by now. Still, his nerves jangled.

Then Juliet tapped him on the back.

He turned warily.

"Excuse me, but today's my first day here, and I don't know anyone. Would you mind sitting with me?"

"O-of c-c-course," he stammered, color creeping up his neck. *I can't believe it! This beautiful woman I'm in love with wants to sit with me.*

Mmm, Juliet thought, *his speaking voice is as yummy as his singing one, honey with just a bit of gravel in it. I can't wait to get to know him better.*

That luncheon was the start of many happy times together. Despite his social anxiety, Liam wasn't shy around Juliet, and he shared his life with her as easily as she shared hers with him.

Juliet forgot all about finding the owner of the earrings, until, on the anniversary of their first date, Liam presented her with a white box, similar to the one still locked inside her pantry.

Opening it, she found a necklace that matched the one-carat studs, and gasped. *"You?"* she said. *"You* left the basket?"

"Yes. And I did 'stalk you', sort of. I saw you at the coffee shop every Saturday morning, but I was too afraid to ask you out, so I just listened to everything you and Nancy talked about. Then I decided to give you a special Easter basket."

"You were the person behind the paper!"

"Yes. I hope you can forgive me and wear the earrings and necklace now. I also have something else for you."

Juliet had barely begun to wrap her head around his confession when Liam suddenly got down on one knee and proposed—with yet another one-carat ring.

"Who are you with all these carats, the Easter Bunny?" Juliet gasped.

"I'll be your Easter Bunny forever, if you say 'yes'," Liam replied. "I love you, Juliet."

"YES! I love you, too, Easter Bunny," Juliet laughed.

No Picnic

[Lara meets her fiancés daughters for the first time when they all go on a picnic. As they approach the area where they will set up, the girls start fighting, and Lara has second thoughts about marrying Devitt. Then they discover that all the food in their cooler has been stolen.]

Lara carried an oversized beach bag downhill to the picnic area by the water's edge, sat atop an empty table, and rested her flip-flopped feet on the bench. She couldn't wait to meet Devitt's daughters; after all, she'd soon be their stepmother.

Ah, there they were! Devitt and three lovely little girls, ranging in age from about five to nine, were coming down the same hill she'd just navigated. Devitt carried a large cooler and each daughter carried a brown grocery bag. The youngest reminded her of Dakota Fanning, same big blue, soulful eyes and blonde hair. The middle one was nearly a carbon copy of her father, and she had his wavy brown curls—a plus. The oldest was sure to be a knockout when she grew up. In fact, it appeared she already was...

Lara's mouth dropped open in shock as she watched her take a big bottle of ketchup out of the bag she carried and whack her unsuspecting middle sister with it.

Pandemonium ensued. Middle Sister dropped her bag and grabbed her head, wailing. Little Sister flung protective arms around Middle Sister and screamed at Oldest Sister, "You hit her! Why did you hit her?" And Devitt glanced desperately around while shushing all of them, obviously hoping his girlfriend hadn't witnessed this most unladylike display. His face fell when he saw Lara, and he hissed something at the girls.

Oh, boy. Lara jumped down from the table intending to make herself scarce before they reached her, but it was too late. Oldest Sister had already skidded down the hill to stand beside her. "Are *you* Lara?" she asked, sniffing with disdain.

Not everyone can be a beauty queen, mean girl, Lara thought. "Yes, I'm Lara."

Just then the others joined them, and Little Sister

said, "You gotta help her! She might have a combustion!"

"That's *concussion*, dummy!" Oldest Sister corrected.

"Yeah, well, you oughta know. You gave it to her!" Little Sister spat back.

"Girls! Girls! This is no way to act in front of my fiancé!" Devitt scolded, setting the cooler down on one end of the table.

Lara emptied a plastic bag that held sunblock, opened the cooler, added ice, and handed it to Middle Sister. "Here, put this on that bump. It'll help the swelling go down."

"Sorry, Lara," Devitt whispered in an aside. "I asked them to be on their best behavior today. I don't know what's gotten into them."

Oldest Sister, that's what. Lara whispered back, "It's fine, Devitt. Kids will be kids. Why don't we all go for a swim? Hopefully, the water will cool a few tempers."

"Okay now, sweet pea?" Devitt asked Middle Sister. When she nodded, he yelled, "Last one in is a rotten fish!" and ran for it. Everyone else zipped after him— except Lara. She walked, uncaring if she got the "smelly" label. No wonder Devitt hadn't introduced her to his brood before. The way they acted would make anyone have second thoughts.

Although the horseplay, splashing and dunking dispelled the girls' sour moods and they *seemed* like normal, happy kids again, Lara remained unconvinced. They'd already shown their dark little underbellies. And Devitt had hidden their existence from her until now, a month away from the wedding, which made her wonder what else he was hiding. Some picnic this was turning out to be!

Swim time over, they headed back. Devitt began to

dump charcoal into the free-standing grill nearby, and Lara started to remove the package of hamburger she'd seen in the cooler earlier, but when she opened the lid, the meat, condiments and two liter bottles of soda had disappeared.

"The meat's gone!" she exclaimed. "And so is everything else, except for the ice."

"What the...?" Devitt bit off, striding over to see for himself. "Alright, which one of you little devils is responsible?" he demanded, brows lowering.

"Dad, none of us did it. We were all in the water with you the whole time," Oldest Sister reminded him. (Lara still didn't know their names.)

Devitt shook his head in dismay. "I'm sorry, Lara. I knew my girls weren't any picnic, but this... this really *is* no picnic."

"Daddy, we're sorry!" the trio cried in unison. "We'll help you find our food. We *want* to have a picnic with Lara. We *like* her."

The girls marched upon their neighboring picnickers. Turned out the man flipping burgers at a nearby grill thought their cooler had been left there by others in his group.

Devitt, Lara and the girls joined them and gorged on twice the goodies. Lara winked in turn at Katelyn, Madelyn, Cherilyn, and their father, her family-to-be. Her attitude had done a 180° turnaround during the meal. The girls really were sweet. And she loved their father. Hooking up with them would be twice the picnic, too.

Moon Dance

[After viewing a total lunar eclipse together, two friends become much more.]

The potluck and dance to benefit the local yoga studio's scholarship program was something Lily had been looking forward to for the last three weeks. She'd just moved here six months ago, so she didn't know many of the residents yet. Lily hoped she would meet some new people at this event.

However, when she arrived at the studio there were only a few people she didn't already know, and they were either much older than she was, or they were too young, especially the little boys running around in the central area that had been cleared for a dance floor. *Oh well,* she told herself, *at least it looks like there's some good food here.*

She set her own dish, a big pot of homemade spaghetti, on the table then went to the other end to pick up a paper plate, napkin and plastic utensils before moving on down the buffet line to choose her own potluck items.

As she snagged a fried chicken breast with her fingers—the fork was too flimsy to use to pick it up—she heard an accented voice behind her say, "Tsk, tsk, tsk, such bad manners!"

Lily pivoted with a retort ready on her tongue, but it got tied when she saw the stranger who had taken her to task. He was tall, easily a foot taller than she was, with sandy blond hair and hazel eyes that were twinkling with undisguised mirth.

"But I won't tell, if you promise to share. You took the last breast piece, and it's my favorite," he accused.

Finding her voice, Lily told him, "Sorry, I don't share my chicken. And I didn't touch any of the other pieces when I got this one, so tattle all you want, neener, neener, neener!" Then she stuck her tongue out at him.

He snorted and said, "I knew you were a juvenile delinquent! Now you owe me a dance, as well as half your chicken."

Laughing, Lily said, "I won't share my chicken with you, but I will let you have my leftover spaghetti at the end of the evening, and I will dance with you after I eat, if that works for you."

"Deal!" he said and followed her through the line to a table with two adjacent empty chairs. He set his stuff down and pulled out one of the chairs for Lily.

"Thank you," Lily said. "You are quite chivalrous when you're not being a stuffed shirt."

"I'm not a stuffed shirt, *yet*, but I plan to be," he replied digging into his food with gusto. He polished off two plates of dinner food then went back for a dessert plate before Lily finished her single dinner plate. And she couldn't help but notice that both of his dinner plates held heaping servings of her spaghetti.

When he sat down with his dessert plate, Lily stared at his slender but sinewy frame and said, "Where do you put it all?"

"Oh, I have two hollow legs," he replied airily.

"Uh-oh, I bet you won't be able to dance now that you've packed them so full," Lily teased.

"Just you watch," he told her popping a last bite of pie into his mouth and standing. He held out a hand to her. The band was playing a slow song, and he led her expertly around the small area.

"What's your name, Punky?" he asked.

"Punky? I'm not Punky; I'm Lily. And what's your name, Stuffy?"

"I'm not Stuffy, but I *am* Duffy."

"Duffy?" Lily giggled. "Really?"

"Short for Lucas James Harris Macduff," Duffy said with a grin.

"Wow! That's a mouthful!"

"And it's even longer when I add 'the third' to the end of my name. Hence, Duffy."

"Well Duffy, thank you for the dinner company and the dance, but I have to work tomorrow, so I guess I'll see you around."

"Don't you owe me some spaghetti?"

"You really want to take home more spaghetti after all you ate here?"

"Of course I do. It's delicious."

Duffy followed Lily back to the buffet table, and she scraped the bottom of the pot for him. There wasn't a lot of spaghetti left. He covered the plate with some tinfoil, said, "Thanks, Punky. See you around," and sauntered out of the studio.

Darn! Why didn't we exchange contact info? Lily thought regretfully. *Guess I'll just have to hope we do see each other around.*

* * *

Lily walked down the hill toward the Christmas festivities. Santa would soon appear in the bell tower of the old school then ride in his sleigh on a float to the town square where he would give out goodie bags to young and old alike. She hadn't seen a celebration like this since she was a very small child, and she knew she would meet more townsfolk here.

As she walked along, someone joined her. When she looked over, who did she see but Duffy, the man who had danced with her back in October at the yoga studio. Her eyebrows rose in surprise. Since she hadn't seen him anywhere in the last couple of months, Lily figured he was just a visitor who'd moved on.

He smiled at her and asked, "Mind if I walk with you?"

"You already are, aren't you?" Lily answered offhandedly.

"Indeed that's true," Duffy agreed, crooking an elbow in an invitation for her to take it.

Lily linked her arm in his, grateful for the extra support going downhill. "So where have you been, Stranger?"

"I've been right here, but since I was too dumb to get your number when I met you, I couldn't call you. I had just stepped out of my door when I saw you walking down the hill. So I assume we both live on this street?"

"You assume correctly, gallant Sir."

"And may I assume that you will give me your number as my reward, Fair Lady?"

"You may, but only if you give me yours, too."

At the bottom of the hill, they joined the throng where Lily laughingly sat on Santa's lap and received an extra bag of goodies which she gave to Duffy. As they milled around the square and talked to the people Lily did know as well as Duffy's friends, he polished off the two bags of goodies.

"My goodness!" Lily exclaimed. "You really do have two hollow legs! And I bet they're only an eighth of the way full. Do you want to come up to my place, and I'll share the leftovers from the dinner party I had last night?"

"Darn! I missed a dinner party? I knew I should have gotten your number sooner."

"Well don't just assume that all I'm going to do is feed you," Lily said unthinkingly then turned beat red when Duffy's eyebrows shot up into his hairline.

He guffawed then said, "Milady, we have just begun to see one another. I intend to court you properly, have no fear."

And from that moment on, that's exactly what Sir Duffy did. He took her to the New Year's Eve dance at the old dancehall, and joined her for New Year's Day dinner at her house, then took her for a scenic drive out in the country later that afternoon.

They came back and sat on his front porch where they had a great view of the sunset. Lily oohed and aahed because it was so spectacular. "I bought this little house just for this front porch," Duffy told her. "I love to watch sunrises, sunsets, and the stars from here."

"I can see why," Lily agreed. "I wish I had the same view you do."

"Milady, you are most welcome to come and enjoy my view anytime you want. In fact, there is a total lunar eclipse coming up on the 21st of this month. Would you like to join me in watching it?"

Lily readily agreed, and on the night of the eclipse, they stood side by side watching it. Until Duffy pulled her up against him, so that her back was against his front, and she was supported. The eclipse lasted two hours, so it was a very good thing Duffy did that.

After an hour and a half in his arms, Lily was halfway in love with him. When he turned her around to face him and danced her across his front yard in the red moonlight, she was three-fourths of the way in love with him. And when Duffy kissed her, his heart totally eclipsed hers.

Blood moon
Eclipsed
By love.

Shari Broyer
© 2-20-2019

The Heart Tree

[When Myra's little boy, Joey, goes missing, she finds him sitting groggily under the overgrown oak tree at the property line. Joey insists the tree is a "heart tree", but Myra has her doubts, especially when new neighbor Michael gives her grief, something she's all too familiar with, over it.]

Myra's little boy went missing. She'd believed he was fast asleep in his bed, but when she went to wake him from his nap, he was gone. Trying not to panic, she searched Joey's room, looking under the bed, in his closet, behind his toy chest—and inside it. No Joey. Calling, "Joey, where are you?" like she did when they played Hide and Seek, Myra combed the entire house, but still no Joey.

She finally found him, outside in the backyard, sitting trance-like a few feet away from the tree next to the fence. Had he been sleepwalking? Myra hurried westward toward the boundary of their property. When she reached him, Myra lightly touched her son's shoulder so as not to startle him. "Joey, wake up honey," she said softly.

"Mommy," he answered groggily, pointing. "Look! It's a heart tree. It means love."

Myra looked at the tree and saw nothing but a scraggly oak with branches overhanging the fence. She really should have it pruned, but finances had been tight, and since the house next door was vacant with no one to complain about it, she hadn't bothered. "Honey, you've been dreaming. That's just a plain old tree. Come on," she said, bending down to pick him up. "Let's go back inside."

But Joey resisted. "No, Mommy, it's a heart tree. Can't you see it?"

"Oh, yes, I do see it now," Myra answered, pretending to scrutinize the oak just to placate him. "Let's go, sweetie. I've got to get back to work, and I need you where I can see you."

"Okay, Mommy. I'm glad you saw the heart. It means love."

"So you've said," Myra responded, shaking her head. That must have been some dream.

* * *

Two weeks later, a moving van pulled up next door. Myra saw it through the living room window under which her desk sat. Uh-oh. She crossed her fingers and hoped she wouldn't have to get that tree serviced just yet. As a medical transcriptionist who worked from home, her pay didn't stretch to extras. At the age of only thirty-three, her husband, Will, had died of a sudden massive heart attack, and she'd been struggling ever since to keep their home and care for their son on her own.

Every now and then she glanced up at the progress in unloading the van while she worked. The third time, her gaze caught and held on someone who could have been Will's twin. His dark hair, brown eyes, and olive skin were the same. So was his build. Fixated now, Myra forgot to type and watched the man's biceps flex as he helped heft a massive chest of drawers from the van and carry it inside.

When he was out of sight, Myra heaved a heavy sigh, arose and closed the drapes then returned to her job. She'd been seeing Will's double everywhere in the year since he'd passed. Now, it was the moving man; next, it would be the homeless guy on the corner downtown.

* * *

There was a sharp tattoo on her front door.

Geez, can't you use the doorbell? Myra grumbled inwardly and pulled herself up from the couch where she'd been cuddling in her pajamas with Joey, watching Saturday morning cartoons with him.

As soon as she opened the door, Will—no, not Will— the moving man, no—whoever it was, backed her up as he surged forward into her home without invitation. "That tree is encroaching on my property, making a mess of my backyard. What are you gonna do about it?" he growled like a grizzly on steroids.

"Come in, make yourself right at home," Myra said smartly. "I'm Myra Culver, and this is my son, Joey. And you are?"

Ignoring her, he barked, "Let me speak with your husband. He needs to get off his duff and take care of the problem."

Fuming—how dared he just barge in and start making demands?—Myra said in a biting tone, "Well now, that might be pretty hard for him to do, seeing as he's dead."

That stopped the rude man in his tracks. He had the grace to look ashamed. "I'm very sorry for your loss," he said in a voice that was several decibels lower. Clearing his throat, he said, "Well, now I understand why the tree's been allowed to grow unpruned. I'll take care of it myself." He turned and started back out the door.

"Wait!" Myra said. "If we're to be neighbors, wouldn't it be good to know each other's names?"

"Uh, yeah. I suppose. I'm Michael Ferrari." He stretched out a massive hand.

Taking it, Myra disregarded the tingle she felt and joked, "Had any speeding tickets lately?"

"Very funny. But as you can probably tell, I'm not built that way."

"No you're not." Myra's eyes traveled that fine build of his, and a blush stained her cheeks when she couldn't help circling the block a second time.

Releasing her hand with a grin that brought out faint dimples in his cheeks, Michael said, "Well, it was nice to meet you, Myra—and Joey."

Joey, who'd been lost in *Looney Tunes* on Nickelodeon replied absently, "Nice to meet you, too," and kept watching the screen.

"He loves his cartoons, especially since he only gets to watch them for a couple hours on Saturdays," Myra explained by way of apology.

"Hey, don't we all?" Michael shrugged and let himself out.

The instant he was gone, Joey jumped up from the couch and ran to Myra. "Mommy, Daddy sent him to us from the heart tree!" he exclaimed, proving he hadn't been as engrossed in the TV as he'd seemed.

"What are you talking about, Joey?" Myra had forgotten all about the heart tree business.

"Daddy's heart, it's in the tree, and he sent Michael to meet us."

"Oh, Joey," was all Myra said as she scooped him up into her arms and headed for the kitchen. "Who wants Happy Face pancakes?"

"I do!" Joey yelled happily.

* * *

A year later, the oak tree's branches had been properly trimmed, for the fourth time, into the shape of a heart. Michael had done this at the behest of Joey, in preparation for their backyard wedding. As Myra surveyed her fiancé's handiwork, she felt a momentary pang of sorrow in her own heart because she'd had to lose one wonderful man in order to gain another. There was now no doubt in her mind that her son had connected with Will in that strange heart tree dream, and she was sure Will had given them his blessing through it.

She whispered, "I'll always love you, Will. Thank you for sending Michael to us."

First Flush of Love

[When hunky maintenance man, Saul, helps Felicity retrieve the keys she believes she accidentally flushed down the toilet, her "flush" deepens.]

"Hey gorgeous, what do you say we duck out of this boring affair and have a more memorable 'affair' of our own?" The dog-faced man had been hounding Felicity ever since she'd arrived at the charity event her boss insisted she attend. Now, Dog-face slung a too-familiar arm around her shoulders which she promptly removed.

Ugh. Time to bolt. "Um, could you please excuse me for just a minute? I have to use the ladies'."

Darting out of the hotel ballroom into the restroom, Felicity found that she actually did need to use the facilities. She entered a stall and completed her business, then hitched up her satiny dress pants. As she did so, she heard a jingle followed by a plop and a whoosh as the automatic flusher kicked in.

"Oh, no!" she wailed.

No way could she execute "operation getaway" now. Going back to that ballroom wasn't an option. If she waited too long, her keys would become a part of the city sewer system, and she didn't have a duplicate set at home—an oversight she'd definitely remedy as soon as she got them back, *if* she got them back.

This was so embarrassing! Why hadn't she put her keys in her clutch instead of her pocket? Then this never would have happened. Oh well... no time to lose.

Jogging up to the concierge's desk, Felicity said, "My car keys got flushed down the toilet. Is there any way to get them out?"

The bored-looking young man stationed there yawned and picked up the phone. "Get me the maintenance supervisor, please."

A minute later he said in the same monotone, "Saul? Come to the main lobby right away. We have an emergency."

You'd never be able to tell it from your tone of voice,

Felicity thought frowning. *Saul will probably take his sweet time, and I'll be saying sayonara to my keys.*

"What's the problem, Levi?" The unexpected question sounding from right behind her made Felicity jump.

She spun around to face a broad chest. Gazing downward, she saw brawny arms and big hands, one of which was holding a tool box. That was fast. Craning her neck, she took in the six-foot-plus height of the man. He sure was quiet for someone so large. His rough-hewn features were somehow handsome. Mmm. Was this the maintenance super? If so, he was "super", all right.

Felicity shook her head. What was she doing mooning at him? Time was of the essence here. She forced herself to focus on the conversation between Levi and Saul.

"This lady's keys got flushed down the toilet in the restroom over there," Levi smirked, "and you get to fish them out for her."

She expected Saul to laugh at her predicament, but he only asked, "When did this happen?"

"About two minutes ago," she answered.

"Can you show me which stall?"

"Follow me."

Felicity went in first to ensure that the restroom was empty. She bent over and checked for feet in the double row of stalls. There were none... except in the very one she'd just vacated.

"Hello?" Felicity called in a panic. If the woman flushed, her keys would go even farther down the plumbing.

"Yes?"

"Please, when you're finished, don't flush!"

"Are you nuts?"

"No. I dropped my keys in that toilet a few minutes ago, and it already flushed once. Maintenance is waiting right outside the door."

Felicity heard the rustle of clothing and then a whoosh.

"Noooo!" she cried.

"So sorry, honey. It did it on its own. I couldn't stop it." The woman stepped out, her expression sympathetic.

When she was gone, Felicity poked her head around the outer door and said glumly, "All clear."

Saul set up a **Restroom is Being Serviced** sandwich sign and entered.

"Why the long face?" he asked.

"That lady was in my stall and the toilet flushed, again!"

"I'll take a look."

Saul emerged seconds later with a big grin on his face, and Felicity couldn't help noticing how attractive it was. From his hand dangled a set of keys.

"Wha...?" Felicity was stunned. Saul couldn't have wielded his plumbing tools that quickly.

"They were on the floor in the stall next door."

"But... I heard them fall into the toilet before it flushed!"

"Did you have anything else in your pocket?"

Come to think of it, she'd jammed both keys and a lipstick hurriedly into her pocket as she left her car earlier. She stuck her hand inside it now, and her face reddened. The plop had been her lipstick.

Saul picked up her free hand. Felicity's skin tingled at his touch. He placed the keys in her palm and smiled, at which Felicity's blush deepened. "That flush on your face is the only thing we need to worry about now."

Felicity's "flush" spread to her neck and chest, and Saul's smile widened. He folded her fingers over the keys and said, "Hmm... How do we fix that, I wonder?"

Boomer

[Delilah, intent on catching her wayward pet, crashes right into Hayden, who hits his head on a rock when they both tumble to the ground. Contrite, Delilah nurses his wound and asks him to join them. Boomer, who was born on the Fourth of July and weirdly likes fireworks, does his "happy dance" when they start, and Delilah's heart does a "happy dance", too.]

"Boomer! Boomer! Come back here Boomer!" Delilah ran after her wayward Airedale terrier. He'd slipped his leash again and was haring across the park after a squirrel. "Darn dog!" Delilah muttered, but she really didn't mean it. Boomer was the best dog, so friendly and smart. He didn't want to hurt the squirrel; he just wanted to play with it.

"Boomer!" she called again. But Boomer wasn't about to be deterred. He really wanted to make friends with that squirrel.

Anxious to catch him before he caught up with the squirrel, Delilah's focus was solely on her dog, so she didn't see the man who had veered in from the side to try to help her, and she ran into him full tilt.

The two humans fell in a heap on the ground while Boomer ran the squirrel up a tree and stood at its base barking.

"I'm so sorry!" Delilah said as she sat up.

"I'm sorry, too," he replied in a disgruntled tone as he also righted himself. "This is what I get for trying to be helpful," he added, gingerly touching an angry-looking knot on his forehead.

"Oh no! Did that happen just now?"

"Yes, it did. Apparently, I hit my head on this rock," he said gesturing toward the object half hidden in the grass. "You really need to have better control over your animal," he scolded. "Have you thought of obedience school?"

"Boomer just started school last week. I didn't think he needed obedience training before, but now that he's older and bigger, he's a bit harder to control. He's a good dog, though, really. It's my fault; I didn't tighten his collar enough, and he slipped out of it."

They stood and brushed themselves off. "I have some ice in my cooler back there," Delilah offered pointing to her picnic blanket.

"Thanks," he said, "but I think we'd better corral Boomer first." He nodded at the dog still barking away at the squirrel.

"Yes, of course," Delilah agreed looking down at the collar and leash she still held in her hand. "I'll catch him and hold him if you would just slip this collar over his head."

"Sounds like a plan," the man said.

So, that's what they did. Once Boomer was back on his leash, the man tightened his collar and walked with them back to their blanket. "My name's Hayden. What's yours?"

"It's Delilah, and you've already met Boomer."

"What made you give him that name?"

"Boomer just happened to have been born on the Fourth of July, and it's also his favorite holiday."

"Really? So today is his birthday? How old is he, and why is it his favorite holiday, besides being his birthday?"

They had reached the blanket, and Delilah motioned for him to sit. After he did so, she and Boomer sat, too. Then she answered his questions, "Boomer is now two years old. And most dogs don't like fireworks, especially the booming kind, but Boomer absolutely loves them. He gets all kinds of excited. If you stick with us until the fireworks start, you'll see."

As soon as the words were out of her mouth, Delilah felt herself grow warm with embarrassment. What was she doing, asking a complete stranger to join them? Even if he was a very handsome one. What if Hayden had his own spot here—one complete with a family, or a girlfriend?

To cover her embarrassment, Delilah busied herself by handing him Boomer's leash and getting to her knees to retrieve some ice from the cooler and put it in a baggie for his head. "I'm sorry, I shouldn't have asked you that."

"What? To stick with you and Boomer until the fireworks start? I'd be happy to, actually. I just came here to walk around and get some fresh air. I wasn't planning to stay for the fireworks. But you and Boomer have made me want to stay. I'm eager to see what Boomer does when they start."

"You might not be so eager then," she said ruefully. But I have a nice picnic I'll share with you to make up for it."

"Sounds like a plan!" Hayden said for the second time.

"You sure are full of plans," Delilah teased.

"I sure am!" he agreed. "And meeting you and Boomer has filled my head with quite a few more."

And you have filled my head with some plans, too, Delilah thought, feeling excitement even though the fireworks hadn't yet started.

Once the swelling had gone down on Hayden's forehead, they were both able to enjoy the picnic of fried chicken, potato salad, baked beans, potato chips, and watermelon that Delilah had packed into the cooler along with Boomer's favorite hot dogs. He loved them cold, and before the evening was over, he would eat the whole pack.

During the picnic, Hayden told Delilah about his profession as a restorative architect and his latest job of bringing the old library—which had been closed for the past fifteen years due to unsafe conditions—back to life.

"What a coincidence!" Delilah exclaimed. "I'm a librarian at the new library, but I used to love going to the old one when I was a kid. The new one just doesn't have the same ambiance. I'd love to work in the restored building, if they're going to keep it a library, that is."

"I'm pretty sure it will still be a library," Hayden told her. "A lot of the old books are still there, covered in dust cloths, and they're not moving them out. My crew and I have to work around them."

"That's so awesome!" Delilah said.

"Yeah, it's the best part of my job, saving historical buildings, especially when they get to keep their original purpose." He set his plate aside and rubbed his tummy. "That was one fantastic picnic," he told her.

"Well I'm glad you liked it, and that you helped me eat it up. I always make way too much because I'm the oldest of five, and I had to do a lot of the cooking since Mom and Dad both had to work to support all of us. I never learned to cook for one, so my freezer is always full of leftovers."

"Mmm, can I come over and help you eat them?"

"Seriously? Yes you can. Or you can come over and help me eat a fresh dinner and take some of the leftovers home for yourself."

"That sounds like a plan!" Hayden said for the third time.

"It sure does!" Delilah agreed, smiling.

Just then, they heard the sound of the first firework shell being launched out over the nearby lake. Boomer did his happy dance, spinning around and around barking and howling.

Hayden threw back his head and howled, too, with laughter.

Delilah giggled and said, "Told you so!" Taking a hot dog out of the pack, she said, "Here Boomer boy! You crazy mutt! This is for your amazing performance!" *And for bringing me and Hayden together.*

Walleyes

[Rod, a man afflicted with congenital monocular exotropia in his left eye, meets Hallie, who also has the condition in her right eye, when he accidentally steps on her foot. Then the couple discover a unique solution to their problem.]

Rod Harris glanced to his right effortlessly. Then he looked to the left, but only his right eye responded, so he didn't have a completely clear view of that side of the street. He started across, and a horn blared at him. There'd been several surgeries to try to correct the congenital monocular exotropia that affected his left eye without success, so he lived as best he could with the condition.

The other thing he lived with was his lack of success with women because of it. Since high school, females had only liked him as a friend and only because he made them laugh. They never considered him as anything more. He would have been handsome had it not been for his eye, but they just couldn't see past it.

Jumping back onto the curb, Rod nearly fell off it again when a woman directly behind him cried, "OUCH! You stepped on my foot! Why don't you look where you're going?"

Rod whirled around which caused blurring in his left eye, but he could still see the extremely pretty woman before him. "Sorry! I would've if I could've, but I was blinded by your beauty."

Hallie Baker was so shocked at being considered "beautiful", her right eye clouded up and so did her brain. She had congenital monocular exotropia in that eye. Boys had teased her mercilessly in school, calling her "Fish-eye Hallie". Now, men just looked away when they saw her; they certainly didn't think she was a "beauty".

When Rod's vision cleared, he noticed—almost at the exact same time that Hallie noticed—they both had exotropia. They stared at each other out of their good eye then burst out laughing. What were the odds?

"Want to come have coffee with me?" Rod asked and added, "IF we can cross the street without getting ourselves killed."

"I've got an idea," Hallie replied. "Have you ever heard of walleyes?"

"Walleyes? Aren't they those fish with both left and right exotropia?"

"That's correct, but actually all fish sort of have our condition. Anyway, what if we combine ourselves into a walleye and cross the street? I can check the right side, and you watch the left."

"Then let's put our heads together!" Rod agreed.

Cheek to cheek, the couple safely crossed and laughed all the way to the coffee shop at the end of the block.

Reluctantly, they separated heads when they reached the door, and Rod held it open for Hallie. They found a table in a back corner after they ordered—black coffee for Rod, mocha latte for Hallie—and talked the Saturday afternoon away.

"Is it really almost five?" Hallie exclaimed as Rod took a last sip of his third cup of coffee and she saw the time on his watch when it protruded out of his sleeve. "I'd better go! I have a dinner to get to."

Rod's face fell. He hadn't enjoyed himself this much in forever, and now it seemed Hallie had a dinner date. Well, she *was* very attractive. Her eye wasn't permanently fixed to the right, the way his was to the left, so she must have the intermittent kind of exotropia. But even when her eye did turn outward, Rod still thought she was pretty.

"Have fun on your date," Rod said glumly as he rose to pull her chair out for her.

Date? Rod thought she was going on a dinner *date*? "Oh, no, no, it's not a date. It's at my friend's house. She and her husband invited me. I'm their daughter's godmother, and it's my once-a-week chance to play with Barbie."

"*Barbie*? They named their daughter after a *doll*?" Rod joked.

"No, silly!" Hallie laughed. "They named her after her grandmother. Her name is Barbara, but I like to call her 'Barbie' and bring her Barbie dolls and accessories. She's seven now, so it's the perfect age for it. We play Barbies, too," she admitted with a grin.

"Do you need 'Ken' to come play with you?" Rod couldn't help but ask. He really wished he could join her. He didn't want this dream day to end.

Hallie dimpled. "Maybe another time, after I've told Christy and Brandon Beauchamp about you. That's okay, isn't it?"

"It's more than okay, pretty lady," Rod said, pulling out his phone. "Can I get your number? Maybe take you out to dinner next week?"

"How about tomorrow, instead?" Hallie suggested. "I can't wait to see you again."

"My thoughts exactly!" Rod agreed.

They swapped contact info and set up a date for the following evening.

When Hallie arrived at Christy and Brandon's house an hour later, she floated into the kitchen with a huge smile on her face. "Christy," she told her friend, "I met the most charming, handsome man today!"

Christy's eyebrows rose. "Oh really? Well, why didn't you bring him with you?"

"I didn't want to just spring him on you. Besides, we barely know each other. When we're farther along in the relationship..."

"... 'Farther along in the relationship'? My! My!"

Christy teased.

"I *hope* it's going to turn into a relationship. I have a dinner date with him tomorrow night."

And it did turn into a relationship. Rod and Hallie were connected at the cheeks for several months, helping each other heal from the wounds of the past as they also assisted each other in navigating the difficulties exotropia caused them.

Rod quickly became a welcome favorite in the Beauchamp household and attended dinner there every Friday night. He and Hallie were grownup "Barbie and Ken" and Barbie was their "daughter" when they played with her after dinner.

After only six months, Rod proposed, and Hallie, of course, said, "YES!" A month later, they had a small backyard wedding at the Beauchamps' place with Christy, Brandon, Barbie and all the dolls in attendance.

The photographer took cheek-to-cheek pictures of them so Rod's more pronounced exotropia wasn't as noticeable. They looked just like any other handsome couple. And they were...

[Author's note: In loving memory of my brother, who had exotropia affecting his left eye and died young, without ever having a special relationship. This one's for you, Bubba.]

The Sweetest Day

[Cyllene meets Jon after she nearly runs him down in the parking lot as she is leaving her job at a candy factory. Then Jon teaches her about a little known Midwestern holiday, and she rewards him "sweetly".]

Cyllene sighed with relief as she got into her Mini Cooper and started it up. Work at the Anthony-Thomas Candy Factory today had been grueling, and it was only the beginning. An order issued from the top said to step up production of their specials, and Cyllene couldn't understand why. It was mid-October. People didn't usually hand out boxes of assorted chocolates for Halloween, which was the next "candy" holiday.

"Oh, well," she said aloud with another sigh. "At least it's a job. Gotta pay the bills." Cyllene talked to herself all the time since there was no one else to talk to. She'd been an only child. Both parents had been killed in an airplane crash shortly after she'd turned 18. Gram, her only other relative, had passed away in her sleep a month ago. She'd left Cyllene the house and all her worldly goods, but she'd also left some debt.

The worst part was, Cyllene hadn't even gotten to know Gram until six months ago. Mom had been estranged from her single mother, so she'd always told Cyllene that Gram was dead. Gram had been searching for her daughter for years when she stumbled upon her granddaughter. Cyllene had changed her last name to Blest—Mom's maiden name, hoping it would bring her better luck than her father's name—Harms—had brought all of them. Cyllene needed some good luck, especially since she'd lost her job of 11 years when the cosmetics company she'd formerly worked for had folded.

From the moment she'd received the invitation to come to Columbus, Ohio and visit her long-lost relative, Cyllene believed her fortune truly had changed. She was "home" the minute she arrived, and her Gram was the sweetest lady who ever lived. Whenever she told her that, Gram always retorted, "No, you are, Cyllene. That's what your name means—'sweetheart'."

Now, the house felt empty, even though it was still

crammed with all Gram's stuff, and her life felt even more hollow than it had before. She didn't want to go there, but she had nowhere else to go. Exhaling heavily for the third time, Cyllene put the Mini in Reverse and started to back out of her parking spot.

"STOP!!!" a man yelled.

Cyllene, who'd been using the camera assist to back up, stopped immediately. She should have remembered to check her surroundings, not just rely on technology. "Oh no! Did I hit someone?" she cried as she hopped out of her car and ran all around it, searching for the injured party.

But no one was there. "What the heck?" she muttered, then flinched when she felt a hand on her shoulder.

"Sorry, I didn't mean to scare you, but you did almost hit me. If I wasn't a 'white man' who *can* 'jump' after playing college basketball..."

Whirling around, Cyllene saw only the front of a man's sweater. She had to look way up to see his face. "Gee, you're tall!" she blurted.

"Yep, all six feet, nine inches of me," he grinned.

"So you couldn't have just stepped over my little Mini?" Cyllene quipped.

"Nope, had to jump sideways, which is luckily one of my patented basketball moves." He grinned again, and Cyllene was smitten. He wasn't textbook handsome, but he had a boyish charm aided and abetted by dimples and wavy brown hair that flopped forward into his big brown eyes.

"So very sorry," Cyllene said seriously.

"I'll tell you what, come have dinner with me, and we'll call it even."

"I don't eat dinner with strangers," Cyllene said, quirking a questioning eyebrow at him.

"Jon Johnson," he stuck out a long-fingered hand, "but you can call me 'Dodge'."

Cyllene giggled and shook his hand. "Good one! Okay, 'Dodge', I'm Cyllene Blest, and I'll have supper with you if you answer three questions."

"Shoot," he said, still holding her hand.

"Where do you work? Not here, 'cause I've never seen you in the factory, yet you are unexpectedly in the parking lot." She tugged until he let go of her tingling fingers.

"I work right behind here, at IBL Freight Brokers. I cut through here to get to my car every day."

"I want to drive, but you're so big. How are you ever going to fit into my Mini?"

"That's two questions," Jon warned her, and shot a pointed look at her Mini. "I'll find a way to fit."

"You will?" Cyllene gaped.

"That's three," Jon smirked.

"Not fair! You tricked me into asking my last question! But okay, I'll go, IF you can actually fit into the Mini."

Jon folded himself up like a pretzel and squeezed himself into the passenger seat. "I wouldn't do this for anyone else," he spoke from behind his knees.

Cyllene laughed again. This was going to be fun.

* * *

They had dinner at Texas Roadhouse. Cyllene was almost afraid to order the steak she was craving, so when Jon paid the check, she expelled a breath she hadn't realized she'd been holding. Her last dinner date had left her with the check.

When they reached the parking lot again, he directed her to a large, school-bus-yellow Hummer.

"Well, you'll have to come pick me up in that next time," Cyllene said, then blushed. "Sorry, I shouldn't have assumed..."

"Yes, you should have, because I intend to see a lot of you in the future, Cyllene Blest." He leaned over awkwardly and kissed her. Now her lips tingled instead of her fingers. "I'll make dinner at my place tomorrow night if you're free. I live in Arlington Pointe Apartments, not too far from here. Do you like hamburgers and potato salad?"

"Yes, I'm free, and yes, I love hamburgers and potato salad," Cyllene replied.

"Good, 'cause hamburgers are about all I know how to cook. The potato salad is pre-made, but it's delicious, you'll see."

* * *

They had a dinner date—usually at one of the fast food places in the area—nearly every night for the next week, and by then Cyllene felt comfortable enough to invite him to her house for dinner Saturday. "I live on Raspberry Run Drive in Brookhollow, first house on your left off Trabue Road. Come over at five. I'll make us something gourmet."

"Can't wait," Jon said, smacking his lips in anticipation.

Jon showed up at her door with wine, flowers and a big box of assorted chocolates from the Anthony-

Thomas factory store.

"What's all this?" Cyllene asked in surprise, taking the gifts he offered.

"You mean you don't know what day this is?" Jon's surprise mirrored her own.

"Our one week anniversary?" she guessed.

"No, because it's actually eight days we've known each other, not one week. Does knowing it's the third Saturday in October help?"

Stumped, Cyllene said, "No... I give. What day is it?"

"You really don't know. How could you not know? Everybody else in Columbus—and in the entire Midwest, for that matter—knows what day this is!" Jon shook his head, astonished.

"Well, I lived in Eugene, Oregon for the first twenty-nine years of my life before moving here six months ago, so I have no idea, Jon." Cyllene was starting to get aggravated.

"And you work at the Anthony-Thomas Candy Factory, yet no one told you what today is?"

"No, Jon, they didn't. All I knew was that we had to up production of assorted chocolates." Cyllene wanted to shove his gifts back at him and push him out the door in her frustration.

"Aww," Jon gathered her into his arms and kissed her. "I'm sorry. I really thought you knew. Happy Sweetest Day, sweetheart."

"Sweetest Day? Today is Sweetest Day?" It was Cyllene's turn to be dumbfounded. "So the whole Midwest gets a second Valentine's Day that the rest of the country knows nothing about? Is that it?"

"Sort of. Back in the early 1920s, 12 confectioners formed a special committee and gave out over 20,000 boxes of candy to newsboys, orphans, old folks, and the poor in Cleveland. The idea was to create a special day to give candy to loved ones. Sweetest Day just didn't catch on everywhere."

"Too bad, but it is nice for us 'Midwestern' women."

"Not only women. Just so you know, men can receive Sweetest Day gifts and chocolates, too."

"Hold on," Cyllene told him. "I'll be right back." She went into the kitchen, put the flowers in water, uncorked the wine, poured two glasses, opened her box of candy, and plated some pieces, then put the wine and candy on a tray and carried it into the living room.

"Here are some sweets for you, sweetest man, and this is the Sweetest Day I've ever had," Cyllene told him, standing on tip-toes to feed him a creamy chocolate caramel.

"Mmm, thank you sweetheart," Jon said, before leaning down to kiss her with the sweetest lips she'd ever tasted.

Bizzy Bea

[Beatrice gives herself a concussion when she runs right into a ladder because she's too "bizzy" to pay attention. Neal is her unwilling caretaker after volunteering to take her to get medical help, not expecting he'd have to do anything more. He is surprised when he finds he doesn't mind it as much as he thought he would.]

[Author's note: The dictionary defines "bizzy" as "an English policeman", but my friend gave this word her own meaning, as well as giving me the idea for this story. Thanks, friend! (You know who you are.)]

* * *

Beatrice skidded into the coffee shop where her friend Anita sat at a table waiting patiently for her. "I'm sorry, Anita!" she said a bit breathlessly. "I was working on a flier for the art show opening this Friday, and I almost forgot all about our coffee date."

"That's okay, Bea," longsuffering Anita said. (She'd frequently been stood up by Bea.) "I know you're busy. You're so busy, it makes me dizzy trying to keep up with you."

"It makes *you* dizzy? My head is whirling with all the things I have to keep track of," Bea retorted as she walked over to the counter to order a mocha latte.

"Hey, I've got a new nickname for you—Bizzy (spelled b-i-z-z-y for busy and dizzy)—Bizzy Bea," Anita joked.

"Very funny," Bea said with a roll of her eyes.

"You can always 'just say no'," Anita told Bea as she finally sat down, well aware that "yes" popped out of her friend's mouth uncensored the second anyone asked her to do anything.

"No, I can't. People count on me, and I don't want to let them down."

"They wouldn't if you didn't volunteer so much," Anita insisted. "You work full time online, fundraise for nearly every charity in town, belong to this club and that; you're on the Arts Council, and you sing in the community choir. Not to mention, you never say 'no' to any invitation. When do you find time to breathe? It's no wonder you're so bizzy!"

"But I love being a part of this community, *and*

volunteering and taking part in all the events I'm invited to!" Bea protested.

"I'm just sayin', girlfriend, if you don't slow down, you're gonna get so bizzy, you're gonna spin out of control and crash."

* * *

Later that same day, Anita's dire prediction came true.

Bea hustled into the gallery to give Marlene the fliers she'd made and printed out. She was in a hurry because she was about to be late for her online work meeting, so she didn't see the ten-foot ladder in front of her. Bea ran smack into it, fell backwards and knocked herself out, also knocking the guy who was replacing a bulb in the high ceiling off of the ladder in the process.

Neal fell right on top of Bea and scrambled to get up before he suffocated the poor woman. "I'm so sorry!" he said.

"Oh-h-h," Bea said, as she came to and put a hand on her head.

"Are you alright?" he asked with concern.

Bea's head swam. "I don't know," she replied. "I'm bizzy."

"'Bizzy'?" Neal said with a frown. "I think you might have a concussion."

That was when Bea realized she'd used Anita's nickname instead of the word "dizzy", which she was, especially when she looked into the man's mesmerizing topaz eyes. Maybe she did have a concussion; she'd never ever seen eyes that color before.

Neal helped her up, holding her steady with an arm around her waist. "Let's get you to a doctor, make sure you're okay."

After examining her and finding a large lump on the back of her head, the doctor at the clinic expressed concern that Bea was most certainly concussed. "Is there someone who can take you home and keep watch over you for the next 24 hours?" he asked.

Her dizziness made her incoherent. She was trying to say she'd call Anita, but it came out, "Call the fairy."

Dr. Kerns said, "Oh, boy," and shook his head, giving Neal—who'd been standing by—a questioning look.

"I'll take her home and see that someone is there," Neal offered with some reluctance. He didn't know the woman, and he really needed to get back to work. There was a lot to get set up before the show a week away.

"Do you know where you live?" Dr. Kerns asked Bea.

Bea mumbled, "Down the street," and pointed.

"Oh, boy," Dr. Kerns said again. "Do you know your name?"

"Bizzy Bea," Bea answered.

The doctor tsked. "We'll look her information up. She's definitely going to need to be watched overnight, and if she worsens, a trip to the hospital for a CT scan will be necessary."

Armed with aftercare instructions and Bea's address, Neal drove her home. "Do you know where the key is?" he asked, assuming she had a spare hidden outside somewhere.

Bea had left her purse in her car back at the gallery because she'd just intended to run in and out, but she did have her keys. She never left her vehicle unlocked. "In here," she said, fumbling for them in her jeans pocket.

Neal breathed a sigh of relief. Bea was starting to make sense again already. He'd get her inside, find her phone, call someone and be on his way.

He helped her to the couch, found some Tylenol to give her, and now she was drowsily resting. Neal hated to bother her, but he really did need to get back. "Bea, where's your phone?" he asked.

"Outside," she answered vaguely.

Maybe she wasn't getting better after all.

Neal searched all over the house, then went outside to check the back patio. No phone. He sighed and ran a hand through his hair. Then he remembered there had been fliers all over the floor and guessed Bea had been delivering them to Marlene.

He called Marlene on his cell phone. She would know someone.

But Marlene was a new volunteer, and she didn't know anything about Bea, except that she was supposed to be coming in with fliers.

Sighing again, he explained the situation and told her, "She needs to be watched, so I guess I'm it. Tell Suzanne I won't be back today, and maybe not tomorrow, either."

Neal kept watch over Bea until the next morning. He spoon fed her a bowl of chicken soup, after which she drifted off to sleep. Concerned, he made sure to wake her every couple of hours and ask her something. Gradually, her answers became more coherent.

Now, at 7:30 a.m., Bea walked out to the kitchen on steady feet, headache almost gone. "Thank you," she said, startling Neal so much that he jerked and some of the coffee in his cup sloshed over.

"You're welcome, and good morning," Neal replied as he recovered. "Would you like a cup?"

"Yes, please."

Neal poured her some coffee from the pot he'd brewed. "How are you feeling?"

"Like I hit my head on a concrete floor, but better than yesterday," Bea said wryly. "Did I knock you off that ladder?" she asked.

"Yes, but I fell on top of you, so I didn't get hurt. Do you hurt anywhere else besides your head?" Neal asked, suddenly worried his weight might have caused Bea another injury.

"No, I'm all right," Bea answered.

Breathing a sigh of relief, Neal looked at her as a woman instead of his "patient" for the first time. She sure was a cutie. Short blonde curls rioted around her heart-shaped face, and big baby blue eyes gazed into his.

You sure are all right, he thought and decided then and there he wanted to get to know her better.

The Lone Wolf

[Lizzie, a wildlife conservationist, tracks an endangered Mexican gray wolf as it heads toward a ranch. Knowing it could be legally shot if it attacks the rancher's cattle, she tries to get Mr. Altaha to allow her to tranquilize it and move it out of the area. When he refuses, Lizzie has no choice but to try to get to the wolf first.]

Lizzie Dosela tracked the lone Mexican gray wolf that prowled around the small Arizona town via her GPS device and the radio attached to his collar. It was unusual for one of these endangered animals to stray so far from its pack. "How did you get here?" Lizzie mused aloud. "More importantly, where are you headed now?"

There was a cattle ranch just outside of town, and Lizzie watched as the signal changed to show the wolf heading in that very direction. "Uh-oh. Not good. You're going to get yourself killed, boy."

She jumped into her jeep and drove toward the ranch, hoping to head the wolf off. If she could get ahead of him, she'd tranq him before he could attack any of the cattle.

But none of the surrounding access roads or washes allowed Lizzie to get close enough to achieve her objective, and there was little time to lose, so she drove right to the ranch and knocked on the front door of the main house.

A powerful-looking man answered. Lizzie could tell he was Apache because she was also Apache, and he had the features of a tribesman. "Yes? What do you want?"

"Mr. uh..."

"Altaha," the man supplied.

Interesting, Lizzie thought. *That name was originally borne by stockmen, and he's a rancher.*

"Mr. Altaha, my name is Lizzie Dosela, and I'm a wildlife conservationist. A lone Mexican gray wolf is headed toward this ranch."

The man's face darkened like an approaching storm. "I'll go get my gun."

"NO! *Please*," Lizzie cried. "That's not why I told you about him! He's endangered."

"Well, he's *endangering* my cattle! I found a mutilated calf just two days ago. I have the right to shoot the wolf, and that's just what I'm going to do!" He slammed the door in Lizzie's face.

Lizzie ran back to her jeep and located the wolf. He was now just a mile away. *Oh, what have I done?* Lizzie castigated herself as she grabbed her kit containing a dart gun and tranquillizers and sprinted off on foot, praying that Mr. Altaha wouldn't catch up to her before she got to the wolf.

When she was within 200 feet, she hid behind a tall rock. The animal approached and began sniffing around. Lizzie sighted him in her dart gun then pulled the trigger. The wolf fell to the ground.

In the same instant, Mr. Altaha appeared with his rifle raised. Lizzie jumped right in front of the wolf and shouted, "NO!!! Don't shoot!"

Growling like he was a wolf himself, the man ordered, "Move out of the way, or I'll shoot *you*!"

Lizzie would have laughed at his audacity if her heart hadn't been pounding so hard. "Mr. Altaha, I'm *not* going to move, and you aren't going to shoot this wolf. I've already tranquilized him, so he'll be out for hours. There's a cage in the back of the jeep I left parked in your driveway. Please go get it. Once the wolf is safely caged, we can carry him back to my jeep, and I will take him away."

"And why should I do that, Miss Dosela? You could still let him loose in the area, and he'd come after my cattle again," the man replied from behind his rifle's sights.

"First of all, what happened to revering this magnificent creature in the way of our tribe? You know as well as I do he symbolizes loyalty, spirituality and community to our people."

"I lost my reverence when he killed my calf," Mr. Altaha said, still holding up the gun.

Lizzie continued listing reasons why the wolf shouldn't be shot. "Second, I'll see that you're reimbursed for the calf. If it were a deer roaming free, you wouldn't have cared, would you? This creature is just doing what comes naturally to him. It's only since men have been corralling animals for food rather than hunting them—as he does—that there's been a problem. Now, there are only 113 Mexican gray wolves in Arizona, 257 total anywhere. Once, they were all over the Southwest."

He shrugged.

"Third," Lizzie added, "I won't be letting him 'loose in the area'. He's been separated from his pack, and the rest of them aren't anywhere near here. I will take him back to his family."

Finally lowering his weapon, Mr. Altaha said, "I'll be back."

"Thank you!" Lizzie called after his retreating back.

* * *

A few days later, after the wolf had been successfully reunited with his pack, Lizzie received a call at the Southwest Wildlife Conservation Center where she worked when not in the field.

"There's a Mr. Altaha on line three for you, Lizzie," the receptionist informed her.

Why in the world is he calling me? Lizzie wondered. *And how did he find me?*

She punched number three on the telephone console and answered, "Lizzie Dosela speaking."

"Miss Dosela, this is Nantan Lupan Altaha."

"Woah!" Lizzie exclaimed. "You mean to tell me that your first name is *Gray Wolf*? Am I seriously hearing you right?"

Lizzie couldn't see it, but Nantan Lupan's face was red.

"Ahem," he cleared his throat. "Yes, yes it is."

"And your last name is *Stockman*?"

"It would seem so," her caller replied, sounding embarrassed.

"Wow! What a contradiction! And what symbolism!"

"Yes. Now, if you're done with name games, Miss *Commoner*, would you like to know why I'm calling?"

"Sorry, of course," Lizzie answered, chastened by Gray Wolf's knowledge concerning the meaning of her last name.

"I'd like to know how the wolf is doing, for one thing."

"He's doing just fine, relocated to the wilderness in one of the national forests near Tucson. And what's the second thing you wanted to know?"

"Well," Gray Wolf paused for several long seconds.

"Yes?" Lizzie finally prompted.

Clearing his throat, Gray Wolf said, "Since you're working in Scottsdale, may I assume you also live there?"

"I'm not sure I want to give out that information, Gray Wolf. First, tell me how you found out where I work."

"It was a matter of elimination. There are only a few centers in the state. I contacted two, and you happened to work at the second place I called."

"Why do you want to know where I live?" Lizzie asked, mollified.

"Because a brave and beautiful woman like yourself—one who puts herself in the path of a weapon to save an animal—intrigues me, and I'd like to get to know you better. Scottsdale's not too far away, so I would like to take you to dinner sometime."

"You would?" Lizzie asked, more than surprised. If she were honest, she'd had several daydreams about his dark good looks since they'd parted ways. Now, it appeared the attraction was mutual. "I happen to know your last name also means 'from a high place'. Are you certain you don't mind being seen with a 'commoner'?"

"Not when she's as lovely and as fiercely loyal as you are," he replied.

"Well said!" Lizzie applauded. "All right. I'll have dinner with you."

After deciding with him where to meet and giving him her personal phone number, she hung up with a smile. This lone wolf wouldn't be alone for long.

Desert Dreams

[An anonymous man comes up behind Isla at a dance and says, "Hello, beautiful." He turns her around, takes her in his arms, dances and sings along to Fleetwood Mac with her, embraces and kisses her, tells her, "I love you," then disappears out of her life.]

Isla walked in the twilight as a balmy breeze — the harbinger of a monsoon on its way to the tiny Arizona town — ran its cool fingers through her hair. Lanterns flickered in the courtyard that was her destination. She could see their light reflecting off their sparkling sequins and the iridescent ribbons they were hung from. She could also hear the music — resonant, hypnotic, blending ancient rhythms with the pulse of the present. The annual Dance in the Desert was underway, and Isla quickened her steps, eager to give herself over to the wildness in her heart.

She came alone, as she often did, but Isla didn't mind dancing by herself or with single friends. She swayed and dipped, twirling through the crowd in a flowing dress the color of moonlight, her auburn hair tumbling over one shoulder, her eyes searching for a friend to dance with.

Then she saw Becca, just as Becca saw her, and the two danced to "Hold Me" by Fleetwood Mac, its lively beat inspiring them to be silly and playful as they held each other's hands, swung their arms back and forth and bounced around on the pounded dirt "floor".

When the dance ended, Becca said, "Whew! I need some water. Want some?"

"Sure," Isla replied and remained where she was while her friend went in search of hydration.

As she stood there, the music shifted and "Dreams" began to play, the opening chords floating above the murmur of conversation, sending a ripple of recognition through the gathering. Isla smiled, remembering her mother humming the tune, "Thunder only happens when it's raining…" She smelled the far-off rain in the air and sang along, an ache of nostalgia in her voice.

Suddenly, Isla felt someone approach her from behind. There was an electric prickle at the nape of her neck. Before she could turn, a warm voice, low and rich, sounded just behind her ear.

"Hello, beautiful."

Her heart gave a little leap as a gentle hand touched her shoulder and spun her around to face him — a man she'd never seen before. He was tall, with dark, curly hair and a smile that held a hint of melancholy. His eyes, a deep, unfathomable brown were shadowed.

"Hi," she said, "I'm Isla, and you are…?"

Wordlessly, he drew her toward him, his palm settling lightly at her waist.

Isla hesitated for a heartbeat, but the magic of the night and the promise in his gaze dissolved all caution. Even though she still didn't know his name, she rested one hand on his shoulder and let him lead her into the allure of the song.

They moved together as if they had always known one another, as though their bodies remembered a choreography from a past life. As Stevie Nicks's voice soared, the stranger began to sing in a smoky tenor that wrapped around the melody and sent a thrill through Isla's core. He crooned the lyrics into her ear: "Thunder only happens when it's raining; players only love you when they're playing…"

"Say women, they will come and they will go-oh-oh," Isla joined in, her high soprano harmonizing with his lower tone.

He spun her slowly, the gauze of her dress flying in the breeze, and when he stopped, his arms were a safe harbor. She laughed, a little breathless.

The lyrics echoed among the crowd as everyone sang,

"When the rain washes you clean, you'll know…"

They continued to sing along, their words a spell they wove together in moments that seemed suspended like desert rain just before a downpour. As the tune drew to a close, Isla sighed and said, "I've always loved this song."

He smiled, a hint of sadness in his eyes. "Me, too. There's truth in it, don't you think?"

"I suppose so," she replied, searching his face. "It always seemed bittersweet to me, like love is just a game that everyone always plays, yet nobody ever wins."

He nodded, his hand tracing gentle circles at the small of her back as they stood close together. "Maybe. Or maybe it's about letting go — accepting that love can be beautiful, even if it's fleeting."

Something in his tone made Isla's heart ache. She wanted to ask his name again and what had brought him to the desert, but the words dissolved on her tongue as the stranger drew her to him, wrapped his arms tightly around her, and put his cheek next to hers. She felt his breath, warm and ragged, as he whispered, "I love you," his voice breaking.

Before Isla could even process his words, he turned his face a fraction, eyes shining with profound emotion, and pressed a soft kiss upon her lips. Then he released her and vanished.

Isla stood rooted in place, the warmth of his embrace and his kiss lingering like phantoms. She turned in a half-circle, scanning the fluctuating throng, but he was gone — swallowed up in the music, the night, and the mystery of the desert itself.

She wandered around in a daze, the refrain looping in her mind: "Thunder only happens when it's raining; players only love you when they're playing..." Had she just been played? Was he a wandering heartbreaker, drifting from town to town, connecting briefly with random women then leaving them longing in his wake? The thought stung, yet there had been tenderness in his touch, and the sorrow in his gaze didn't seem like that of a "player".

As the night deepened, Isla found herself rerunning their encounter, searching for clues. His presence had felt familiar, almost fated, but she knew neither his name, nor his story.

Becca returned with their waters and asked, "Who were you dancing with? I don't think I've seen him around here before."

"I don't know," Isla replied, shrugging. "Just some random guy, I guess. Come on, let's dance."

Isla tried to make herself believe what she told her friend, and she tried to have fun, but everything seemed hollow, the enchantment of the evening gone like a disappearing dream.

The desert moon climbed higher as Isla made her way back home alone. Sleep eluded her for a long time, and when she finally did drift off, she dreamed of mysterious brown eyes and the song she would never be able to forget.

* * *

Morning brought no answers. Isla walked through the town searching for his face. She even asked around, describing him to several of her friends, but no one seemed to have seen the man. He might as well have been a ghost.

By the day's end, Isla's heart was raw, resigned. "Maybe he'll come again next year," one friend suggested. Isla managed a wistful smile, but her hope of ever seeing him again was already fading.

* * *

A month passed. Then two. Life returned to its regular rhythm. Isla's days were filled with work and her evenings with the ache of memory. She couldn't shake the feeling that their encounter meant more than just a dance and a kiss.

Then, one afternoon, a thick envelope arrived in her mailbox, postmarked from a city in California. Inside was a brief note along with another envelope.

The note was typed and read, "My friend was able to track you down, after some searching, due to your unusual first name. He's no longer with us, but he wanted you to have this."

Isla gasped in shock, and a stabbing pain seared her heart.

With trembling fingers and eyes blurring with tears, Isla tore open the second envelope to find a handwritten letter and a photograph inside.

Dear Isla, the letter read:

I hope this letter finds you well, and that you're not too angry with me for disappearing the way I did. You deserve better than a mystery; you deserve the truth. There's so much to explain, and so little time…

I'm writing because I need you to know that dance with you meant everything to me. I've been sick for a while — really sick — and the doctors say my time is short.

I wasn't supposed to be in Arizona — my family worried — but I wanted one last adventure, one last experience of what it feels like to really live. When I saw you, so radiant under those desert lights, I felt bliss for the first time in ages. Dancing with you, singing that song — it was as if all my pain, fear, and regret melted away.

I said "I love you" because, in that moment, I did. Not the way most people mean it, perhaps, but with all the gratitude and wonder a heart can hold.

I didn't want to burden you with my story or make you pity me. I wanted you to remember that night as something beautiful, not as a goodbye. You are unforgettable. Thank you for dancing with me, a stranger. Thank you for letting me be, for a few cherished minutes, someone who still believed in "dreams".

Dance, my darling, don't ever stop, and look for me in the music, in the balmy breeze, and in the thunder that only happens when it's raining.

With love, always,
Your "Player"

The photograph was of the two of them. Someone had captured them mid-spin beneath the lanterns, joy radiating in their smiles. How he'd gotten it, she would never know.

Isla wept, holding the letter and photo to her wounded heart. What he'd said about the song made sense now. He hadn't been a player in the cavalier way she'd feared, but rather, he had been playing for time, for meaning, for one last embrace.

After that, whenever Isla heard "Dreams," it wasn't regret that filled her, but gratitude. She remembered how the stranger's arms had felt around her, how his voice had meshed with hers, and how she had learned from him that sometimes, the most precious love is the kind that lingers for just a few moments, then disappears—leaving you changed, and more alive, than ever before.

A Haunting Refrain

[Lenore is going crazy because a certain song is being played over and over wherever she goes. So, when she gets home after a particularly trying day to hear it being played yet again—loudly—by her next door neighbor, she loses it. Pounding on his door, she orders Raven to "Turn it down!" and soon finds herself haunted by something other than the song.]

"I'll make you see
That it's a thriller, thriller night
Cause I can thrill you more than any ghost would
Dare to try
Girl, this is thriller, thriller night
So let me hold you tight and share a killer, diller
Chiller
Thriller here tonight!"

~Final refrain from Michael Jackson's *Thriller* (1982)

* * *

Lenore, named after the girl who died a tragic young death in Edgar Allen Poe's poem, couldn't get the *Thriller* refrain out of her head. It circled around and around like buzzards over roadkill. It didn't help that Halloween was just around the corner, and the local radio station played the old eighties song seemingly every hour. Wherever Lenore went, she heard the song, and that last chorus jumped out at her each time.

"Grr..." Lenore growled, gritting her teeth as the song played in the Save A Lot. *Like I have a man to hold and thrill me. This song is just taunting me—no, it's* **haunting** *me.* She almost ran around the store, rushing to gather all the items on her list before it played again.

When she arrived home from shopping, Lenore began to unload her groceries... until she heard the darned refrain coming from the house next door. "Enough!" she cried aloud then stomped across her yard and up the neighbor's steps to pound on his door.

Lenore had never met the man, though he'd moved in four months ago. He was always gone. Except for today, when she was already driven to madness by the stupid song. He just *had* to be home now; he just *had* to be playing *Thriller*. She was less than thrilled.

When he opened his door, Lenore rudely yelled, "TURN IT DOWN!", whirled around and clomped back down his steps.

"Turn what down?" Raven called after her, perplexed. When Lenore only slammed her front door shut in answer, he shrugged and kept listening to his favorite Halloween video while he put up decorations.

"Guess *she* won't be coming by for treats on Halloween," he told Spooky, his black cat. "Although it's a shame, really. She's pretty cute when she's not mad."

An hour later, Raven finished putting out spider webs and bats, pumpkins and jack-o-lanterns, headstones and skeletons, and turned the video off.

Lenore, who had donned her swimming earplugs in self-defense, didn't hear when Raven rapped on her front door. She kept cooking her solitary supper—beef teriyaki with green peppers, onions and rice.

Getting no answer to his knock, but finding the front door unlocked, Raven poked his head inside and called, "Hello? Hello? Anyone home?"

Still no answer, but Raven could smell something good wafting from the kitchen, so he ventured further inside, still calling "Hello?"

Lenore looked up and screamed at the unexpected sight of him standing in her kitchen doorframe.

"What are you doing in my house?" she demanded when she could speak coherently.

"I knocked, but you didn't hear me," he answered.

"What?" Lenore had forgotten she still wore the earplugs.

"I said..."

Shaking her head, Lenore thought, *It's finally happened; hearing that song so much has made me deaf.*

Then she remembered the plugs. Taking them out, she said sheepishly, "Sorry, what was that?"

"Why are you wearing earplugs?" Raven asked instead of answering her initial question.

Lenore glared at him. "Because you won't quit playing that stupid song!"

"What, you don't like *Thriller*?"

"No, I don't like *Thriller*!" she yelled. "Especially when it's being played at a hundred decibels, and I asked you to turn it down!" Lenore waved the knife she was using to chop green peppers at him.

"Whoa, lady!" Raven said, backing up a step with his palms out. "Let's not get crazy now."

Lenore realized she'd been brandishing her knife at him and hastily put it down, blushing. "Sorry. But hearing that song over and over does make me crazy, and you're not helping. Why wouldn't you turn it down?"

"Maybe because you didn't ask; you ordered me to turn it down?" Raven posited then cleared his throat when he saw her face darken. *This isn't gonna win you any points,* he told himself. "Ahem, but it's off now, and if it bothers you that much, I won't play it so loud in the future."

"Good. So, why are you here?"

"I came over to ask if you wanted to have dinner with me. I was gonna grill some steaks, but I see that you're already cooking your dinner." Raven put on his puppy dog face, hoping she'd get the hint and ask him to share.

"Yes, I am," she said pointing to the front door.

"Okay, well, maybe another time. Name's Raven, by the way. What's yours?"

"Lenore," she bit off.

"Lenore...your parents were Poe fans, too?"

"My mother, if you must know."

"Both my parents," Raven said with a deprecating shrug. "It really bothered me when I was a kid. The others teased me saying, 'Nevermore can you play with us!' and stuff like that. But as an adult, I find my name fits, especially since I do have jet black hair."

Drawn into the conversation despite herself, Lenore responded, "Most of the kids I knew didn't realize 'Lenore' was a Poe poem. They just heckled me because it's so old-fashioned—'Lenore is a bore! Lenore, snore!' Stuff like that. I'm still not too keen on it."

"I think it's a beautiful name..." Raven said, leaving "for a beautiful lady" unspoken.

But Lenore got it, and she blushed again. She really was cute.

"Well..." Lenore began.

"Well," Raven cut in. "I'll just take myself out of your pretty caramel-colored hair now."

Blushing a third time, Lenore said, "No, I wasn't going to ask you to leave. I was going to ask you to join me."

"Great!" Raven crowed. "What can I do to help?"

* * *

By the time Halloween rolled around two weeks later, Lenore and Raven had grown a lot closer. And once the trick-or-treaters left the neighborhood, Raven had a special treat just for Lenore.

He had his Vincent Price collector's set with Edgar Allen Poe's "Tales of Terror", "The Pit and the Pendulum" and "The Raven" at the ready on the DVD player. He had also popped some corn and filled two glasses with fizzy cranberry-lemonade-ginger ale punch then put on his *Thriller* video for starters.

Gathering Lenore close to him on the couch, he crooned the last refrain of the song into her ear:

"I'll make you see
That it's a thriller, thriller night
Cause I can thrill you more than any ghost would
Dare to try
Girl, this is thriller, thriller night
So let me hold you tight and share a killer, diller
Chiller
Thriller here tonight!"

No longer haunted by the song but shivering deliciously, Lenore said, "*You* thrill me, Raven."

Million Dollar Goofball

[Carson comes off as goofy when he and Daisy first meet, but he is very serious about her and makes many earnest gestures to prove it. Eight months after they meet, he wants to marry Daisy, but his certainty frightens her so much she ends their relationship. Then Carson calls her seven months after their breakup, wanting to know if he should marry another woman.]

Carson was the kind of guy who laughed with his whole body — shoulders shaking, eyes crinkling, belly heaving. He wore loafers without socks even though the rest of his attire was business casual. And he never minded that he was often the butt of his friends' jokes.

When Daisy first met him at the local roadhouse, those friends were razzing him unmercifully about his inability to shoot a deer.

"Wittle baby was afraid to shoot the gun!" "Wittle baby ran away!" "Wittle baby needs to wear this bib!" And they tied a Red Lobster bib around his neck while he just laughed and took it. (Daisy found out later that Carson wasn't a hunter at all; he just wanted to come up into the foothills, enjoy the scenery, and hang out with his friends.)

When the country rock band began to play, Carson, who had been eyeing her for the better part of an hour, swaggered up to Daisy with a grin that was all mischief. "I'll try not to step on your toes, if you'll dance with me," he said.

"Now that's an offer I *should* refuse!" Daisy laughed as she stood and took his hand. It turned out Carson was a fantastic dancer and knew all the line dances including the Boot Scootin' Boogie. He was also proficient at the two step, the waltz, and the Cowboy Cha Cha, and he whirled her around the floor until she was dizzy, keeping up a stream of hysterical banter all the while.

Still, beneath all his goofiness, there was a certainty to Carson. He knew what he wanted — a rarity in Daisy's life at the time. He called her the next day, and every day thereafter for the next week.

When she confessed her fondness for theater, he drove three hours from the Bay Area to her small rented cabin in the Sierra Nevada foothills the following weekend to take her to dinner at a restaurant in a nearby preserved gold rush town.

There, in addition to dinner, local actors presented a murder mystery, and all the patrons had to help solve it — a perfect start to the Halloween season.

Their courtship was a parade of earnest gestures, most notable of which was the fact that Carson made the long drive to see her nearly every weekend without complaint. So at Thanksgiving, Daisy drove to his house in Fremont on the Wednesday before, her car loaded with a turkey and all the trimmings plus an apple and a pumpkin pie. When Carson saw what she had brought, he laughed and swung her around gleefully. "You're the best, Baby!" he told her.

At Christmastime, he invited her to his company's party — a million dollar affair held in a San Francisco ballroom with shivering crystal chandeliers and gold-dusted linens. Carson worked for a tech giant, so everything seemed fantastic to Daisy, especially when a very famous singer performed just a few feet away, his voice echoing around the massive room.

Daisy had dressed for the occasion in a stunning new gown, her hair upswept into a French braid, and she felt like a princess — until she saw how beautiful and sophisticated all the other women there were.

But Carson only had eyes for Daisy. He grinned at her and sang a silly, off-key version of "All I Want For Christmas Is You". Then Daisy felt like she was the luckiest person in the city.

For her birthday, he whisked her away to Las Vegas. They stayed at a hotel with neon curtains and a rooftop pool. Carson bought tickets to a dinner show that featured a live performance by a singing duo that Daisy had always loved, and afterward, they watched the colored fountains at the Bellagio, fingers entwined, their laughter rising above the clamor of the Strip.

Carson insisted on going up the Pacific Coast instead of

driving her home after their delightful weekend. "Call your boss and tell her you need to take a few vacation days. She knows it's your birthday, so she shouldn't mind," he urged, so she did. They spent most of the next day at Hearst Castle, where Daisy marveled at the enormous indoor Roman pool, its blue walls and ceilings accented with real gold. Then they wound their way up cliffs and cypress groves to Carmel where they ate Dirty Harry steaks at Clint Eastwood's Hog's Breath Inn and stayed the night at the Carmel Mission Inn.

After poking around the town for a while the next morning, they drove to Monterey Bay and took the scenic 17-Mile Drive, after which they visited the Monterey Bay Aquarium. At sunset, they watched sea otters tumble in the kelp and ate salted caramel ice cream cones. Of course, Carson couldn't resist rubbing her nose with his!

But, as perfect as it all seemed, Daisy found herself pressed down by the weight of Carson's certainty. After only eight months, he said, "I can see a future for us together. I'm ready to settle down."

Daisy still felt unfinished — her dreams meandered. She wasn't sure if she wanted to live in the Bay or the hills, if she was meant for someone so clear-eyed and steady. She told him, "I'm sorry, Carson, but I'm just not ready. Maybe it's best if we stop seeing each other."

Their breakup was gentle, yet messy. Carson tried to joke about it, but Daisy heard the tremor in his voice as he said, "Guess *you're* still a 'wittle baby', huh?" The reminder of the first night they met nearly broke Daisy.

A week later, Daisy received a letter from him that she didn't read for many months.

Time moved on. Daisy finished her Master's degree and began to teach Creative Writing at a nearby community college. She hiked alone on weekends. Sometimes, on those early Saturday mornings, she'd pass a car on the winding mountain road that looked like Carson's, and her heart leapt unbidden in her chest. Carson's company was often in the news — growing, always growing, and Daisy couldn't help keeping informed about it. She wondered if he still didn't wear socks.

Seven months after their breakup, Daisy's phone rang as she stood in her kitchen, watching autumn leaves drift past the window. His number was still in her contacts — she'd never brought herself to delete it.

"Daisy?" Carson's voice was at once familiar and strange. "Hey. I hope this isn't — well, I hope it's okay to call."

She swallowed. "Hi, Carson. Of course, it's okay."

They talked around the edges of things: her new job, his latest tech project, the weather in the city and in the mountains. Then, quietly, Carson said, "I'm seeing someone. Her name's Miranda. She's — she's great." He described her in some detail then said, "We get along. I... I think I might ask her to marry me."

Daisy's stomach lurched, but she managed to say, "That's wonderful, Carson. You always wanted that. I'm happy for you."

There was a pause. "But before I ask her, I guess... I wanted to know if you had any reason why I shouldn't. If I should wait. If you... If things were different for you now."

Daisy heard the hope in his voice, soft and uncertain. She thought of the long drives, the laughter, the warmth of his hand around hers. She thought of why she'd let him go — her fear, her restlessness, her worry she'd never be enough for someone who already knew who he was.

But it was too late. It wasn't fair of her to reinsert herself into his life now.

"Carson," she said, her voice as steady as she could make it, "I give you my blessing. Marry Miranda. You deserve to be happy."

A shaky exhale came over the line. "Thank you, Daisy."

They said their goodbyes. Daisy stood by the window, the phone cold in her hand. She'd meant it, hadn't she? Miranda sounded kind and reassuring, and Carson deserved steadfast love. Daisy had nothing to offer but distance and old doubts.

But as the days passed, regret gnawed at her. She couldn't shake the memory of Carson's goofy laughter, the way he'd matched his steps to hers on every trail they'd hiked together, the protective curl of his arm around her shoulders. She realized with a pang that she'd been waiting for her own certainty, to feel the kind of love that Carson had already given her.

As winter blanketed the foothills, Daisy found herself reaching for Carson's letter at last. The ink was smudged where his tears had fallen. He'd written, "I hope, whatever you choose to do, you feel brave. I hope, if you ever think of me, it's with kindness. I hope you realize I would have waited for you."

Daisy dialed his number. She didn't know what she would say if Miranda answered, or if Carson's voice would sound different this time, colder, more distant.

He picked up on the first ring. "Hello?"

A thousand apologies tangled in her chest. She spoke through them without preamble. "Carson. I was wrong. I do have a reason why you shouldn't marry Miranda... I still love you. I want us to be together again, if you do."

Silence spun out between them, long and brittle. When he finally answered, his joyful laughter hovered just beneath the warmth in his voice. "I broke up with Miranda right after I called you. I never stopped loving you, Daisy. And I'm still ready, if you are."

"I am," she confirmed. "You may be a goofball, but I wouldn't trade you for a million dollars — or another million-dollar Christmas party, although that *was* wonderful."

Outside, the early snow melted from the pines as the sun kissed their branches. In the fragile, golden hush between seasons, Daisy smiled, certain at last.

Love on Aisle 7

[Jane plans to cook a Thanksgiving dinner for her family to prove to them that she isn't a flake. She mistakes a man dressed in a short-sleeved dress shirt and tie for the peasant/store manager and asks him where the stuffing is. Then she cremates her pies and decides, at the last minute, to buy a ready-made dinner. However, the store is all out. Jane is distraught until the knight in shining armor/architect she thought was the manager comes to her rescue by offering to share his ready-made dinner.]

Jane rounded the corner on aisle 7, scanning the shelves and muttering, "Where in the world is the stuffing?" No turkey was complete without stuffing, even she knew that. Intent on her quest, she narrowly missed ramming into the store manager.

Yanking her cart to a halt inches from the guy in a short-sleeved dress shirt and tie she exclaimed, "Oh, good! Can you tell me where the stuffing is?"

"It's on aisle 9," he told her, his indigo eyes beneath black brows twinkling, the dimples that bracketed his full, sensuous lips deepening as he grinned, but Jane didn't notice.

"Thanks," she said and scuttled off. So much to do and only three days to do it in. She'd invited the family for Thanksgiving so she could prove them wrong about her "flightiness". Playing house ought to do it. The only thing better would be presenting them with a steady boyfriend, but she wasn't in the market for another relationship after her last fiasco.

Shifting into domestic mode was easier said than done, though. On the surface, she knew she did appear scattered—her apartment was a chaotic mess—but she knew where things were. It was just that she had better things to do than organize. Like write her novels, attend conferences and meet with creative friends.

Well, time to bite the bullet. Jane located the stuffing with a sigh of relief, paid for it and her other purchases and headed home.

After a day of grueling effort, the apartment was de-cluttered, but Jane wasn't certain she'd ever find the important stuff again, having shoved various stacks of notes into one big box in the closet. She did the mountain of dishes in the sink, swept, mopped, dusted and vacuumed then went to wash grimy windows only to discover she was out of cleaner. Back to the supermarket she went.

Straightening from the low shelf with product in hand, she saw the manager at the end of the aisle and called, "Hey, thanks for helping me the other day."

His smile was wide, his eyes appreciative. "No problem."

This time, Jane did notice. He sure was hot for a supermarket supervisor. That smile was killer. And the way his biceps bulged out of his shirtsleeves... *Focus, Jane,* she scolded. *Get a grip. No more men, remember? Plus, he's a store manager. He wouldn't be your type in a million years.*

"Well...uh...thanks again," she stammered. Executing a hasty turn that almost knocked over a display of air fresheners, Jane hurried away, face flaming while she stood in line to pay for the window cleaner. As she got into her car, she forced all thoughts of him out of her mind.

The next day, Jane cut veggies and did all she could ahead so she wouldn't be tied to the kitchen on Thanksgiving. After pre-heating the oven, she popped two frozen pies into it—one pumpkin, one apple. Then she figured she'd earned the right to work on the story her muse had presented her with in a dream last night.

Sitting at her computer, she spun a medieval tale of a trapped princess and her rescuer, a peasant man with raven hair, deep blue eyes, dimpled smile and sculpted body. As the plot emerged and the characters developed, time fell away.

Then the smoke detector went berserk and black clouds billowed into her little office area in the living room.

"The pies! Oh, no-o-o-o!" Jane wailed. Coughing, she ran to open the back door so the smoke could escape, then darted to the kitchen to pull the charred remains from the oven before grabbing a broom to depress the off button on the deafening alarm.

Jane sank down on the couch and hung her head in despair. What was she thinking? She'd never pull this off. The turkey would no doubt get cremated, too, and her family would smirk in self-righteous complacency. Then, her muse, who'd gotten her into this mess in the first place, provided her with a great way out.

She brought to Jane's mind the ready-cooked turkey dinner in the meat and deli section. It would cost more and stretch her meager budget, but if they still had one, it was worth it. Jane raced back to the store.

"Sorry, we're out," the deli worker informed her.

"Can't you make another one? This is an emergency!"

"Abby, I've got this." The hunky manager appeared like magic at Jane's side.

Turning to her, he asked, "Want to share? I shop here often, and I bought the last Redi-Meal yesterday."

"Braden's a great customer," gray-haired Abby endorsed him. "And an architect—he designed the town's new commerce center. He's also a super nice guy."

Why not? Jane thought. *The family won't believe it. I met a wonderful man on aisle 7 who's now my date and is providing Thanksgiving dinner. I can hardly believe it myself!* It appeared her peasant/"manager" was really a knight in shining armor/architect. Who knew? All she knew was she was never going to make assumptions again.

Birthday Kiss

[Steve, newly graduated from high school, and her cousin Mark's friend, kisses Abby at her sixteenth birthday party. He gives her a locket, tells her he'll always remember her and leaves without explanation. Mark later tells her Steve is joining the Navy, and Abby, who has always had a crush on him, is heartbroken. She wears the locket until she goes to college, but she never hears from Steve again. Until—he shows up at her surprise thirty-second birthday party sixteen years later.]

Sixteen years ago:

Abby's sixteenth birthday party was a smash. All her friends from school had showed up, and her neighbor, Arvin, who played guitar and sang, had come too, even though he was five years older than everyone else. He was her buddy and was happy to provide the entertainment.

They were all standing around him and singing along to a popular song when her cousin Mark and his friends crashed the party. They were all seniors who went to a different school and had just graduated. It was okay, though, because Mark also played and sang, and he had brought his guitar with him, so it doubled the fun.

Abby's heart beat faster when she saw that Steve was among Mark's friends. She'd fallen in love with Steve when she was thirteen and he was fifteen, but he had never looked at her that way, more like she was a tag-along puppy dog whenever Mark included her in the things they did.

Now, she was surprised when Steve walked up to her and wished her "Happy Birthday" then pulled a present from behind his back.

"For me?" she asked inanely, then blushed. Of course. it was for her.

"Yes it's for you," Steve said with a smile, and Abby's heart tripped over itself. She could hardly believe he had brought her a gift.

"Open it," he urged, so Abby sat down on a nearby chair and tore the wrapping off the small package. Inside was a heart-shaped locket on a delicate gold chain.

"Oh, thank you!" she breathed. "It's beautiful."

"I'm glad you like it," Steve said, "but that's not the only present I have for you. Can you come outside with me for a minute?" he asked.

"Okay," Abby said. Placing the necklace back in its box and setting it on a nearby table with her other gifts, Abby fell into step behind him.

As soon as they were out the door, Steve took her hand in his and drew her along with him until they were standing beside his car, a vintage 1957 Chevrolet that Abby had always thought was extremely cool.

The early summer night was balmy, and the full moon smiled serenely down upon them. "I can't stay," Steve told her. "But I also want to give you this." He placed his finger beneath her chin and tilted her face up so that he could give her a sweet, lingering kiss. Then he said, "I'll always remember you, Abby. Have a wonderful rest of your birthday and a great life." Then he got into his car and drove off.

Abby put her fingertips to her tingling lips. *How strange*, she thought. *It's almost like Steve was saying goodbye.*

Later that night, as the party was winding down and her cousin was putting his guitar back in its case, she asked him, "Mark, is Steve leaving?"

"Yeah," Mark told her. "He signed up for the Navy, and he leaves for boot camp at the naval station in Illinois tomorrow."

"Oh," Abby said, her heart sinking. She had hoped that the present and the kiss meant Steve finally wanted to make her his girlfriend, but he didn't even tell her he was joining the Navy, or that he was leaving. She sighed. *Well, I guess that's that,* she thought sadly.

After everyone had gone, Abby gathered all her gifts and took them into her bedroom to put them away.

Sitting on her bed, Abby lifted the necklace out of its box carefully. Then she opened the locket and almost cried to see that Steve had placed a tiny picture of himself on one side of the locket and one of her on the other side. *He must have gotten this picture of me from Mark,* she thought. "Looks like you don't want me to forget you, either, Steve," she said aloud.

Sixteen years later:

Abby was cleaning out her closet and found a box way in the back that she didn't remember putting there. It was filled with memorabilia from childhood, pictures of friends in grade and high school, old cards and letters, etcetera. There was also a small box. When she opened it, she found the locket that Steve had given her on her sixteenth birthday, and she was suddenly awash in memories.

She hadn't thought about Steve in a very long time, although it had taken her several years to forget him after he left the way he did. She'd worn the locket every day until she left for college, just praying that Steve would somehow magically reappear in her life. But he never did.

College was a whole new world for Abby, and she forgot all about the guy who had kissed her and left her high and dry when she met the guy who would later become her husband in one of her classes.

Eli was a wonderful person, and an awesome father to their daughter, Kaylee, and their son, Kyle. Abby still couldn't believe he was no longer with them. He'd been killed in a plane crash two years ago, yet she still swore she saw him walking down the street, and when the phone rang. she still expected it to be Eli on the other end of the line. She was lost without him.

Her thirty-second birthday was nearing, but Abby didn't have the heart to celebrate it. The kids wanted to throw her a party and she told them no, she was just going to get a pizza and veg out on the couch, maybe watch an old movie.

So Abby was flummoxed when she came home from work on her birthday to find her friends and family waiting for her, the house decorated, a cake on the counter, and presents piled high on the loveseat. "Surprise!" they all yelled.

But the biggest surprise was the stranger in their midst. He was very handsome, very muscular, and seemed very interested in her. His eyes gleamed as he gazed at her. Something about the way he kept looking at her seemed familiar, but Abby still couldn't place him.

Then Mark said, "Abby, don't you know who this is?"

"No," she said, shaking her head. "No, I don't know who that is."

"It's Steve!" Mark said. "He finally had enough of the Navy, and he just retired after sixteen years."

So what? Am I supposed to care? It was all Abby could do to keep from voicing her sentiments out loud.

"Congratulations on your retirement," Abby said drily and turned away from him to receive the hugs everybody else was waiting to give her.

For the rest of the evening, Abby did her best to ignore Steve. Who did he think he was, waltzing back into her life as if no time had passed, as if he hadn't just abandoned her all those years ago? At least Eli hadn't deliberately left her.

But Steve didn't seem to care that she wasn't paying him any attention. He remained quietly in the background until almost everyone had left. Then he came up to her and asked, "Abby, could I speak to you outside please?"

Shades of déjà vu! Not again! "No Steve," she answered him rudely, "I think you should leave."

"Please?" he asked quietly.

"Why? So you can kiss me and walk out of my life for another sixteen years? I don't think so," Abby said and held the front door open pointedly.

"I owe you an explanation. Don't you want to hear it?"

"No!" Abby nearly shouted and made a sweeping gesture toward the open door. "Now, please leave."

"Is there a problem, Sis?" Her brother Larry asked as he walked into the living room.

"No," Steve replied for her. "I was just leaving." And he walked out the door.

As soon as Abby closed the door behind him, she regretted it. Reopening it, she called, "Steve! Wait!"

Steve was halfway down the block headed toward his '57 Chevy, but he halted in his tracks then spun around and jogged back to where Abby stood on the sidewalk, arms folded across her chest.

When he reached her, she said, "Alright, talk."

Steve said haltingly, "I-I was going to tell you that I signed up for the Navy and ask you to wait for me. I planned to serve four years, get out and go to college on the GI Bill so I could support you."

"Support me?" Abby echoed, thunderstruck.

Steve swallowed visibly and continued, "Yes, Abby. I wanted to marry you, but I was just a poor dumb guy who didn't deserve you. That's why I never tried to go out with you. I knew I wasn't good enough for you, but I wanted to be."

Abby stood there gaping while Steve forged on with his explanation.

"Then I had my physical, and they discovered I was sterile."

Abby's eyes widened in shock.

"But they said I passed; it wouldn't keep me from serving." Steve gulped again. "But it *would* keep me from making my dreams come true. I couldn't expect you not to want children or have a normal married life. That's why I left like I did, even though it killed me. I loved you Abby; I still do."

Tears rolled down Abby's cheeks as she said, "I loved you too, Steve. Ever since I was thirteen and we met for the first time. It's so sad that you felt you couldn't even ask me out, and sadder still that you felt you had to leave rather than tell me what was wrong. I'm not heartless; I think I would have understood, but you didn't even give me the chance."

"Would it really have changed anything in the long run? I wanted to have a family with you. At least this way, you got to have children of your own. And they are beautiful."

Abby reached up and stroked Steve's cheek. "Oh Steve, you really were a 'poor dumb guy'. We could have adopted. But, I guess you were right. I did get to have a wonderful marriage for ten years and two fabulous kids. I loved Eli with all my heart. I still miss him every day. But I still love you, too. And now there's no reason for us not to be together."

Steve's groan was a mixture of pent-up agony and ecstasy as he gathered Abby into his arms and gave her another sweet, lingering birthday kiss. "I'll never leave you again," he promised.

The Christmas Game

[Emma is overburdened because hubby Josh isn't.
Ever since he got laid off from his programming job
at a major software company, he's done nothing but
play video games, one after another, while Emma
works and comes home to complete all the
household tasks he leaves undone. She gets fed up
and locks him out of the house, telling him, "I need
a partner, not a child." Then Josh redeems himself
in a surprising way.]

"Why can't you listen to me?" Emma complained.

"I'm listening," Josh replied, but he was engrossed in that stupid video game for teens again. It figured, he acted like an adolescent most of the time, anyway. Once, Emma had found his happy-go-lucky approach to life an endearing counterpoint to her own overly serious one, but now it was infuriating. Two years, and the honeymoon was definitely over.

"Josh!" Emma raised her voice. "I said, I need you to come help unload the car!"

"Alright, in a minute. After I get to the next level and save this."

"Now, Josh! I've got too much to do to wait around for you."

Part of the reason Emma was so overburdened was because Josh wasn't. Ever since he'd been laid off from his programming job at a major software company, he'd done nothing but play video games, one after another, while Emma worked and came home to complete all the tasks he wouldn't. Well, she'd had enough.

Storming into the den, she stood in front of the big screen and yelled, "Josh, either you come help me RIGHT NOW, or you'll be sorry!"

"Oh, stop acting like my mother and move out of the way." Josh didn't seem at all fazed by her threat. He had a big surprise coming...BIG.

Later that night, Emma finally coaxed—actually ranted about his irresponsibility for so long he couldn't take it anymore—Josh into taking out the trash. He leapt out of bed and stomped down the stairs in his pajamas and slippers.

Emma felt self-righteous glee as she crept after him and locked the back door behind him. Then she ran and locked the others, too. When he hollered, "Emma, let me in!" she said, in a dead calm tone loud enough for him to hear, "No, Josh. I'm done. Go home to your mama since all you want to do is be a kid and play your little video games. You've been laid off for six months now, and you haven't applied for one lousy job. I'm the one who's been working to make the house payments and pay all our other bills, and I'm the one who's been taking care of all the other things while you've been acting like a little boy."

"Emma, if you'll just let me in, I can explain," came Josh's muffled plea from the other side of the door.

"Nope. I need a partner, not a child. Christmas is two days away, and I can't even get you to help me put up the tree, much less decorate it." Emma's voice broke as she said the words. She was so tired and dispirited. "Have a good life, Josh." She went upstairs and put in earplugs so she wouldn't have to listen to him bellowing and pounding on the door.

When she got up the next morning, Josh was gone. He must have walked to his parents' house five miles away. *Fine*, she told herself, but it wasn't fine. All day long at work, she had to force herself to focus so she wouldn't make a mistake that could get her fired, and it felt like there was a ragged hole in her heart.

When she got home, Josh still wasn't there. She thought he would have remembered where the spare key was hidden and let himself back in by now. So what if he stayed away! Hadn't she told him to go? She was better off without him, anyway. Wasn't she?

But it felt strange and lonely to attend her annual office Christmas party without him the next evening. Afterward, she sat in the car and sobbed, remembering things she didn't want to, especially the time he wrote the Honey Do list: "Love me, love me, love me..." and hid it in the toe of her shoe. Something in there had irritated her all day, and when she finally yanked the shoe off and shook it, the tiny piece of paper had fluttered out.

She did love him; she just couldn't see how they were going to make it.

Sighing, Emma wiped her eyes and drove home. As she pulled into the driveway, she noticed lights she hadn't left on shining through the windows. She took out her cell to call 911 but put it away again because Josh stood in the doorway.

Inside, the tree was up, the lights were hung, and it was decorated. A huge pile of gifts lay underneath it. When Emma stared in disbelief, Josh drew her into his arms. "Now, will you let me tell you that the game I've been playing was one I designed and sold? I was just getting the last bugs out the other night. The royalties will more than make up for our lost income. I'm sorry I didn't help more, but I was on a deadline to turn it in. I didn't tell you about it because I wanted to surprise you."

Emma hugged and kissed him. "You definitely did that. Guess I'll have to let you stay, now. Merry Christmas, game boy."

Santa's Lap

[Tommi, a retirement home activities director, hops up on Santa's lap to try to encourage the oldsters to do the same. But she also has a secondary motive of her own and hands him a letter. When Frank, AKA Santa, reads it, he is motivated to make Tommi's Christmas wish come true.]

At the retirement home Christmas party, Tommi, ever the gung-ho activities director, hopped up on Santa's lap to get the old folks to follow suit. They never seemed to want to do much of anything, and Tommi was always trying to motivate them to enjoy themselves more. Her job depended on it.

My, but Santa had some solid, very muscular legs for someone so fat. And his cheeks were much more chiseled than she expected. He must have been working out.

"Well, hello, cutie," Santa said from beneath his fake beard. "And have you been a good girl this year?"

An imp possessed her, and she whispered into his ear, "Nope. I've been VERY bad."

A twinkle lit Santa's cerulean blue eyes and he laughed. "Ho, ho, ho! Well, then, I'll talk to *you* later."

Before Tommi climbed down, she handed Santa a letter in a sealed red envelope. "This is my request. I hope you can fulfill it," she winked.

Santa took the envelope and tucked it inside his red jacket, right next to his heart. "I promise to give it my utmost consideration," he replied and winked back.

Tommi grinned and reluctantly left his lap. It was the first male contact she'd had with anyone under the age of sixty-five in two years, and she'd enjoyed the little flirtation. She wished she knew who was in that costume, but the agency that sent him over said he'd asked to remain anonymous, as all good Santa's helpers should.

"Alright everyone, come line up and get your picture taken with Santa," Tommi called out once she was standing again.

Nobody moved. "Come on now," she coaxed. "If you sit on Santa's lap, he'll give you a special treat."

That got them moving. They sure liked their treats. The cook at the home was notoriously bad and always managed to burn or otherwise ruin every dessert, so they were eager to receive any goodie that came from outside the place. In this case, the treat was a Christmas baggie filled with a half-dozen assorted homemade cookies for each of them baked by Tommi herself in her off hours this past week.

After they'd gotten their treats, the residents livened up and even joined in the caroling when a trio of Tommi's women friends—dubbed "The Holly Berries" for this celebration but otherwise known locally as The Blythe Trio—arrived. The girls played drums, keyboard and guitar and sang old Christmas favorites.

Throughout the next hour, each and every resident took a turn on Santa's lap, and Tommi couldn't help but feel sorry for him. Some of them were quite hefty, and despite his good, strong pair of legs, that had to be mighty uncomfortable.

Every now and then, Tommi glanced over at him sitting by the Christmas tree, and each time she did, their eyes met. After a while, her cheeks grew red and she stopped looking his way. She wondered what he would think of her letter.

* * *

When Frank got home that evening and took off the jacket of his Santa suit, a letter fluttered to the floor. He picked it up and grinned. He'd completely forgotten that the babe at the retirement home had given it to him, probably for a lark. Curious as to what she might have written—her name and phone number, perhaps?—he tore it open.

Dear Santa,

*I lied. I've actually been an extremely good
girl this year. I've worked hard to make the lives
of the old folks brighter, and I've also done
fundraising for several local charities in my spare
time.*

*That's my problem, you see. I have too much
spare time because I have no one in my life to
help me fill it up.*

*So, dear Santa, if I could have only one wish
for Christmas this year, I'd like a really nice guy
to come into my life. I know that's probably not
in your bag, but I thought it couldn't hurt to ask,
anyway.*

*Love,
Tommi
P.S. I'll leave some milk and cookies out for you,
just in case.*

As Frank finished reading Tommi's letter, a big smile
spread over his face. He had her first name now, and he knew
where she worked, so it shouldn't be that hard to get a phone
number and address for her. This was one present he could
definitely deliver, and he hoped she liked it.

But things didn't go as smoothly as Frank thought they
would. The receptionist in the office at the retirement home
refused to provide Tommi's personal info, and he didn't want
to come out and ask Tommi herself due to the surprise factor.
He wanted to show up unexpected at her door on Christmas
Eve and ask her out.

He tried searching the Internet, but without a last name,
he was unable to turn her up.

So, Frank reluctantly resorted to following her, hoping she

wouldn't catch him and think him a stalker. He waited in the parking lot the next Monday — which happened to be one of his days off — until he saw Tommi emerge from the building, get into her car, and pull out. But not long after he started to tail her, a dog ran into the street in front of his Toyota pickup. He slammed on his brakes to avoid hitting the mangy cur, and that few seconds when his attention was off Tommi's nondescript sedan caused him to lose her.

Undaunted, Frank returned to the retirement office immediately. Flashing his best smile at the receptionist who only frowned at him in return, he asked, "I don't suppose you could at least tell me what Tommi's days off are?"

The receptionist's frown deepened and her eyes filled with suspicion. "I don't know why you wanna know, but she's off on Sundays and Tuesdays. How that's gonna help you get next to her, I can't even guess, but you'd better not try anything funny, or I'll report you to the police."

The next day, Tuesday, Frank called in to the agency, said he was sick, and hung out at the retirement home, hoping one of the residents would know Tommi's last name or phone number or where she lived. He talked to several of them with no luck. Christmas Eve was now less than a week away. He just had to find out where she lived this upcoming Sunday, because Monday was it.

Determinedly, Frank redoubled his efforts on Sunday when Tommi wasn't around to catch him interrogating the residents. After asking more of them about her, Frank finally got lucky.

An old woman who'd had a stroke and was presumed to be mute got gabby as he assisted her to her room. She told him in a garbled voice what Tommi's last name was and where she lived. Frank was unaware that the white-haired lady just happened to be Tommi's grandmother, Vivien.

Vivien smiled crookedly as the handsome young man sprinted off.

The next day, Christmas Eve, Frank showed up at Tommi's door armed with a bouquet of roses tied with green ribbon strung with candy canes.

* * *

When Tommi opened her door to see a strange man standing there with flowers, she almost slammed it shut on him. However, the twinkle in his vivid blue eyes reminded her of someone. "Santa?" she asked.

"Told you I'd talk to you later. How 'good' have you been?"

Tommi grinned impudently. "That's for me to know and you to find out. Did you come here to fulfill my wish?"

"Definitely," Frank said, holding out the flowers. "So, how about dinner? Afterward, you can invite me in and sit on my lap, if you like."

A Last Love Story

[Bestselling author Frances Fulton meets Vietnam War veteran Darrell Danford after he emails her seeking a copy of her out-of-print book. Both are living in retirement communities, and both have afflictions that they discover when they have dinner together. However, neither of them is bothered by the other's imperfections. To the contrary, they are highly attracted to each other, and Frances finds herself ready, at long last, to write one more story.]

Frances was surprised to find an email with the subject: *From Ashes to Accolades*, the title of her bestselling novel, in her inbox. Her book told the tale of a Viet Nam vet struggling with war wounds and PTSD. It had been out of print for years. She had believed her old website was long defunct, too, but evidently, it was not. The site was the only place where her personal email address might have been found online. The sender must have gotten it from there.

Curious, she opened the email to see who still remembered her book after all this time.

As was her habit, Frances glanced first at the signature of the sender. Beneath his name, he'd typed: Veterans Hospital. The poor man. He must have been wounded and was now living in one of the VA facilities.

In the body of the email, Darrel Danford simply stated he had lost his copy in a recent move and wanted to know if it was still available anywhere.

Frances assumed he'd tried the link to the book on her website and had come up empty. She hit Reply and typed:

Dear Mr. Danford,

I'm sorry, but *From Ashes to Accolades* has been out of print for over 15 years. Since you're a veteran, I'll make an exception and send you a copy from my personal stash, if you will send me a check for $30 to cover the cost of the book and shipping.

I am always pleased to hear from my readers, particularly from one who recalls what I consider to be my masterpiece.

I've added my contact information to my auto signature below for your use.

Hope to hear from you soon.

Sincerely,

Frances Fulton

The moment she hit Send, Frances panicked. Why had she sent a complete stranger her home address and phone number? *Because you no longer have a separate shipping address, that's why* she reminded herself. *Hopefully, the man isn't an axe murderer. And you need that $30 because you haven't sold any books under your pen name in months. Nor have you written anything new in months.*

Apparently, Darrel Danford wasn't an axe murderer. Frances received an almost immediate response, thanking her and saying the check was in the mail.

Within three days, she had the check in hand, but Darrel's home address wasn't at any VA Hospital. He lived in an area of Phoenix that wasn't too far from her own 55+ subdivision. Hmm. It made Frances feel a bit strange to discover that. She shrugged it off, packaged the book, and sent it to him.

Another three days later, Frances received an email from Darrel profusely thanking her. "I'm shedding tears of joy to be reunited with the story that helped me through my own struggles with PTSD. Thank you from the bottom of my heart."

The next day, there was yet another email from him that read:

Dear Ms. Fulton:

I'm hoping this isn't too forward of me. I couldn't help but notice you don't live too far from me, also in a 55+ community. If you, too, are single, would you like to have dinner with me? There's a wonderful restaurant right here on the grounds.

If you need my address again, here it is. (He typed it in, along with the name and address of the restaurant.) Attached is a recent picture, so you'll recognize me should you decide to say yes. I anxiously await your reply.

His photo was dated within the month. He was a very nice-looking older gentleman. Frances chewed on her lower lip and debated. She'd been divorced for 20 years and was quite happy being single. She hadn't had a date in a long while now, but she had awesome men friends who sat and talked with her at potlucks, danced with her at the dances, played cards and other games with her at the clubhouse, etcetera. She hadn't lacked for male attention. Did she really need a date?

Frances downloaded and enlarged Darrel's photo then took another look. There were shadows in his eyes at this close range. She could sense he'd lived with great pain, as had her father, whom she'd immortalized in *From Ashes to Accolades*. Daddy had been wounded in the Korean war, but to protect his identity, she'd changed the war to Viet Nam.

Darrel's eyes were magnets she couldn't resist, so she replied she'd meet him for dinner, but he shouldn't consider it a date, just two people with common ground sharing a meal together.

He responded with, "Shall we meet at the community restaurant tomorrow evening at six? I'll wait on the bench outside for you. I have a very good idea of what you look like, but just in case you've changed drastically from the photo on your book jacket, what will you be wearing?"

* * *

As Frances approached the entrance to the restaurant the next evening, Darrel rose from the bench he'd been sitting on. When she reached him, he smiled and took her arm. "You have only grown more lovely with the passing of time," he told her.

Frances blushed. "Well, I can't say the same for you, since I've just met you, Darrel, but your picture doesn't do you justice. You are an exceedingly handsome man."

As they walked inside, she barely noticed his limp, or the burn scars revealed when his shirtsleeve rode up. And she hoped he wouldn't notice the thalidomide fingers on both her hands, a birth defect she'd risen above by becoming an incredibly fast typist, author, and illustrator, despite her missing joints. They were each survivors in their own ways.

Over dinner, Frances asked, "Why did you write 'Veterans Hospital' below your name in your email? It made me think you lived in one. I only answered because of that."

"Oh, sorry for the confusion," Darrel said looking embarrassed. "I volunteer part-time at the local VA hospital. Have done so ever since I recovered from my Viet Nam war wounds. Guess I should have added 'Volunteer'."

He cleared his throat and said, "I hope it won't bother you if I ask this, but what happened to your fingers?"

"My mother was prescribed thalidomide for her morning sickness when she was pregnant with me back in 1960. (I know, I'm giving away my age.) Thalidomide caused serious deformities in over 10,000 children, and a lot of miscarriages, too. I was one of the lucky ones, actually. If you go online and look it up, you'll see pictures of babies far worse off than I was. But, I've managed to overcome my disability for the most part."

"It had to have been hard, though," Darrel said with great understanding.

"It was, but so must have been your experiences, yet

you've gone on to help many others. I never did that."

"Yes, you did. Don't you realize your writing has been a gift to thousands of people? How else would your book have become a number one New York Times Bestseller? I personally can attest to its healing power."

Then old pain was forgotten as they swapped silly stories and laughed until their sides ached. "I hope all this laughing doesn't give me a stomachache," Frances said before popping another bite of chicken marsala into her mouth.

"I sure wouldn't want you to get sick on your first date with me!" Darrel said, unhesitatingly covering her free hand with his own.

"I thought we'd agreed this wouldn't be a date," Frances protested weakly.

"*I* didn't agree to anything of the sort," Darrel insisted. "And I think we're going to have many more dates, Ms. Fulton, because I've admired you since I first read *From Ashes to Accolades*. You have an amazing talent. And now that I've met you, I admire you even more," he added, a wealth of meaning in his tone.

Frances blushed but didn't say anything. She also hoped they'd have many more dates, and she already "admired" him, too. She'd had a string of failed relationships, a terrible marriage, and had remained steadfastly single ever since. Now, thanks to Darrel, she felt it was time to shed her self-protective shell and allow herself to write one last love story.

About the Author

Gayle Leigh Gwinn is the pen name of a bestselling author who now desires to write in a genre other than what she became known for. Gayle is one of her given names, and Gwinn is the last name of her great-grandmother.

Gayle is a romantic at heart and has always wanted to be a romance writer. Her first completed romance novel had some success, so she began several other romance novels, but when her short story in another genre took off, she felt led to keep writing in that area.

Now, Gayle returns to romance with this collection of flash fiction sweet romance stories. She plans to finish the many novel-length romances she has started and self-publish them for her readers' enjoyment. She hopes you won't hesitate to contact her and give her your feedback. Reach her at: **shariannegaylee@gmail.com**.

www.ingramcontent.com/pod-product-compliance
Lightning Source LLC
Chambersburg PA
CBHW060115260626
47160CB00005B/1899